THE DESOLATE
WORLD

KORTNEY KEISEL

First edition February 2023

Cover design by Seventh Star Art

Map design by Foreign Worlds Cartography

www.kortneykeisel.com

For Jen Anderson

You have probably told more people that I'm an author than I have.
Thanks for always embarrassing me in a crowd.

NORTHLAND

Northwater

Cold Mountain

North Palace

Kenmare

ENDERLIN

Enderlin Castle

Dakotaland

Government Center

Camgrove

Axville

Portlake

NEW

TOLSTEN

HOPE

Tolsten House

Lakerlain

Oakefor

Ruler's Palace

Vassel

APPA

Wellenbreck

ALBION

Kearney

Dacoma

Ruler's Mansion

Calicristole

Southcove

CRISTOLE

Cristole Castle

Colonias

Post-Desolation

Distance in Miles

0   200   400

2020

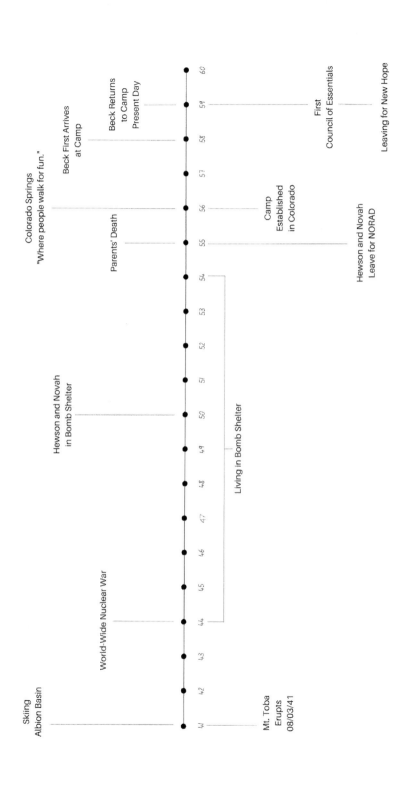

Novah

*On the benches of the Cheyenne Mountains, Colorado
Beginning of Summer 2059 - Present Day*

F ierce wind swirled around *Novah's light-brown hair,
whipping strands into her face and mouth, blinding her
vision. She struggled to breathe. Her lungs filled to capacity with the
strong current of air the tornado created. She cradled the crying baby
against her chest and hovered against the wall.*

"Shh. It will all be over soon," *she said over the whooshing
noise.*

"Novah! Give me your hand!" *She turned her head to her mother's voice. Her arms reached out to her, competing against the tornado's wrath. Fear etched across her mother's brow, but she was
determined to get to her daughter despite the violent wind.*

"Madison!" *her father yelled, wrapping his arms around her
mother's waist and pulling her back.* "It's too late."

Time was running out. Novah felt the urgency of the

moment. *The crying grew louder and louder, matching the intensity of the wind. She lifted the baby up like a kite and let go, watching the wind take it as if it were a tumbleweed in the desert.*

"It's over now," Novah reassured as the baby's wails faded into the funnel.

Then, she turned to her parents. They hovered above her, hand in hand, in the tornado's epicenter.

Her father shook his head. "You should've listened to Hewson."

His disapproving face was the last thing she saw before they were sucked away into a greenish-black hole.

"I'm sorry!" She reached her hand out even though they were gone.

The wind stopped.

Everything stilled.

Hewson stood over her, eyes burning with accusation. "How could you, Novah? This is all your fault." His gaze flickered to her foot. "You got what you deserved."

She followed his stare. Her foot dangled from her leg, swaying back and forth.

Novah screamed, jolting awake. Her heart knocked against her chest, and she looked around, orienting herself.

She was alone in the cave.

Sunlight shone through the opening.

Supplies were stacked neatly together in the corner.

Damp clothes hung on a string beside her to dry.

The mattress she sat on creaked with each heavy breath.

"It was just a dream," she whispered to herself. She closed her eyes, wiping at the sweat on her forehead. "Just a dream."

It had been a while since she'd had a dream where she witnessed the death of her parents. There were different versions and different scenarios, but the crying, the howling wind, and the end result were always the same—they died, and it was all her fault.

She had recurring dreams about Beck, too. Not him dying, but her rejecting him—the same anguish in his eyes. Each dream ripped her heart out in different ways, which was odd since she'd sworn there was nothing left inside her that cared anymore.

When she was a child, people had made dreams seem so whimsical, but as an adult, they'd become nightmares.

Novah rolled off the frayed mattress Hewson had found for her in the wreckage a few miles away, slowly hoisting herself to her feet. The familiar pain in her foot throbbed to life as she gently put weight on it. It always took a second after sitting or lying for long periods of time for Novah to get the injured ankle moving again.

"It's just another day in paradise." She winced as she took a step, ruining the sarcasm in her words. The pressure of the dream would linger with her for the next few hours despite the half-hearted pep talk.

The afternoon sun blared through the cave entrance, beckoning as if it knew she needed something bright to overtake the darkness eating up her mind. She walked to the opening, scanning the camp. Everything looked normal—whatever normal was anymore.

The camp wasn't much, but it was the best they could do in their circumstances. Despite the broken furniture and the dirt they lived with, it was well kept—a home among the ashes of humanity.

Small fires spread out in patches across the mountain bench, releasing billows of smoke toward the sky. The smell of charred vegetables cooking reminded Novah of the ever-growing hunger pains taking residency in her stomach. A few scraps of fabric were tied together and strung between four large sticks, creating a shade canopy. There were tattered sofas and chairs throughout the base—things people had found and carried to camp to make the place more comfortable. Tables were missing legs and propped up with boulders or other crates found in the rummage. Couches missed cushions, and springs punched their way through the thin covers. Piles of random items were separated out, leaning against rocks. There was an "office supply" stack with books and a pile of pens poised on top. Pots and pans were scattered around the "kitchen" area. A few hair brushes and broken pieces of mirrors made up the "personal care" items. Everything was mismatched and makeshift. The place looked like a giant junkyard, except these items weren't junk to the survivors. They were invaluable. Anything new or exciting that was found would be divided among the three camps that were nestled into the benches and caverns of the Cheyenne Mountains.

"I told you to sleep longer." Hewson's strong voice vibrated off the mountain rocks behind her.

Novah turned to see her brother coming toward her, arms full, holding a water basin. With each step, drops of liquid spilled over the edge, splashing on the dirt below.

It was Hewson's idea that she nap in the middle of the afternoon. He always told her she looked tired and weak. But Novah didn't feel weak. She didn't *feel* anything.

Becoming numb was key to her survival.

Hewson, on the other hand, would never be considered weak. He looked rougher than he did from their childhood—no longer carefree and full of life, and no longer a boy. He was almost thirty. He needed a haircut. His brown hair was long, curling over his ears, neck, and down below his eyebrows, brushing against his dark lashes. He was tall and strong. It was a wonder how he'd managed to stay so muscular when there was little food.

"Where is everyone?" she asked, looking around the empty camp. She would've expected at least one person to be roaming around.

"I don't know why it's so quiet. That's why you should've taken advantage and kept sleeping."

"I had another dream," Novah replied in defense, following him as she spoke. She didn't need to clarify that it was a dream about their parents and not Beck since she'd never told Hewson about those dreams and never would. It would only cause conflict. And for what? She'd made her choice a year ago, and now she had to live with the consequences.

Hewson's stern expression faded to concern. "What happened this time?"

"Just the usual." Novah ran her hands down the sides of her jeans, trying to keep her emotion at bay. "It was windy, and there was a baby."

"There's always a baby." Hewson placed the basin in the shade next to other bowls of collected water. "I don't know why you keep letting your mind torture you like that."

He said it as if the nightmares were Novah's fault.

He straightened, hands on his hips. "You need to make new memories."

Novah nodded, grabbing at the sides of her flannel button-up and pulling it around her torso as if the fabric could protect her from the pain. "Yeah, I know."

Excited shouts from the edge of camp stole their attention. Novah squinted into the distance. Fists raised high in the air, and people slapped each other's backs as they looked beyond the field to the valley below. That was where everyone had gone to.

"They made it!" voices cheered. "Drew and Beck made it!"

Hewson's eyes faded to their usual intensity, and he glanced at her—almost like a warning—before breaking into a run.

Beck was back.

Relief seeped through Novah's chest, but she wouldn't believe it until she saw his face.

She ran, too, as much as she could with her foot. Her breaths came fast and were coated with hisses of pain, but she didn't stop.

Beck was back.

Her stomach flipped over just thinking about him. She hadn't seen Beck Haslett since the day he and Drew had left in search of survivors along what was left of the East Coast. She had felt a mixture of disappointment and relief when Beck's hand had shot up a little over a year ago, volunteering to lead the search. Beck had looked at her with a passion in his eyes that had terrified and thrilled her at the same time. He was polarizing, and so were Novah's feelings for him. Hewson hadn't complained about his volunteering to go. He'd hated Beck from the day he arrived at camp a year and a half ago.

Maybe it was because everybody loved Beck, including Novah. He'd walked into camp like he'd just stepped out of a movie—handsome and manly and full of addicting happiness and confidence.

Novah could still remember every detail of his arrival. Until that day, she'd never seen a man whose looks alone could make her heart pound.

Novah

Spring 2058 - A Year and a Half Ago

NOVAH CRAWLED BESIDE the row of holes, dragging her foot behind her. She threw zucchini seeds in each hole as she passed. The sun was warm on her arms and the back of her neck. A sunburn would be inevitable for her fair skin, but she didn't care. Hewson had told her to wear long sleeves to protect her skin, but there was something about the warm rays tickling her skin that helped her feel normal, even for just an hour.

Danny Jakes stood beside her, clutching the handle of his shovel. A few years ago, in another life, Danny and his wife, Emily, had owned a successful ranch in Montana, but a wildfire took his land and his wife from him. He was older than most people at camp, in his late sixties, but his work ethic and know-how made him a vital part of their survival.

"Well, I'll be!" His other hand went to the rim of his cowboy hat, tipping it up. "Who in the Sam Hill is that?"

Novah glanced up, following Danny's gaze. An outline of a man with a large group of people behind him walked up the hill toward the field where they were planting. There had to be a crowd of at least one hundred and fifty people, but the man in front was clearly the leader. She straightened to a kneeling position, using the palm of her hand to shield the sun from her eyes.

The man in front was young, probably around Hewson's age, and handsome. So handsome that Novah leaned forward, trying to get a better look. A big smile spread across his lips as he approached like he didn't have a care in the world, like he hadn't just lived through the worst nineteen years in the history of humankind. He held a bag made out of a floral shower curtain over one shoulder, and his other arm swung confidently beside him as he walked. A plaid shirt was tied around his waist, and he wore a plain white t-shirt and aviator sunglasses, of all things.

Danny threw his shovel down and walked to greet them, calling over his shoulder. "Someone go get Hewson."

Wes, one of the teens, immediately ran back to camp. He was probably happy for any excuse not to work anymore.

"Where y'all come from, son?" Danny reached his hand out.

"All over." The man shook Danny's hand. "I started in North Carolina and picked up people along the way. Drew, here"—he gestured to the man beside him, a shorter guy with a dark beard and a tattoo around his wrist—"heard a radio broadcast a couple of years ago for any survivors to go to NORAD in Colorado Springs. We figured it was worth a shot. So here we are." He pushed his dirty-blond hair back from his face, but one strand kept falling onto his forehead.

"Well, whoever sent that broadcast is long gone. An earthquake destroyed the mountain bunker. Boulders block where the entrance once was. But everyone who heard the radio call found their way here and has been making a home on the benches of the mountain for the last few years. I'm Danny." He tipped his cowboy hat at them before turning and sweeping his arms to the people planting. "And these are just a few of the survivors. There's more back at camp. Actually, things have gotten so full we just opened up a second camp a half mile away."

"This is as good of a home as any." His smile widened, reaching animated eyes. "We're happy to finally be here. We can stay, right?"

"Of course!" Danny slapped him on his back, leading him forward. "Let's get y'all settled between the two camps."

Novah slowly stood as they walked toward her. She shoved what was left of the zucchini seeds into her pocket and dusted her hands off on the sides of her pants.

The corner of his mouth hitched upward even higher. "Beck Haslett." He extended his hand out, waiting for her to shake it.

"Novah Harper." Her fingers slowly brushed against his. Callouses covered his skin, but the warmness from his touch felt as good as the hot sun on her skin.

Beck's hazel eyes glimmered. "Well, Novah Harper,

I'm starting to think coming here was the best decision I've ever made."

She dropped his hand, folding her arms across her chest. "You'll be safe here." That's what she told every newcomer when they arrived. She didn't know if she believed it, but she was still alive, so she supposed it was true.

The glimmer in his gaze flared again. "I'm not sure my heart will be safe." His smile took on a charming quality, as if flirting with a woman was his sixth sense.

"Uh…" Novah stepped back, unsure how to respond. Her heel fell into one of the holes, and she stumbled onto her bad foot.

Beck's hand shot out, grabbing her waist to steady her. She felt the imprint of each of his fingers on her body, and the heat of that touch was enough to burn. How was that even possible? She'd known him for two seconds.

She wiggled out of his embrace, finding solid footing. "Thanks. I've got it."

"Oh, no." He smiled as she shrunk away. "Don't tell me you're already taken. Who is he?" Beck asked playfully. "I'll fight him for your heart."

"Looks like you'll be fighting me." Hewson stepped forward. His chest puffed out, and his eyes hardened. He placed a protective arm around Novah's shoulder, but Beck's smile didn't falter.

"So, you're my competition for the beautiful woman?"

Beautiful woman?

Novah wasn't naive to the fact that she might be pretty. She had big brown eyes and matching brown hair that seemed to wave in a good way without any hair care products that women used to have. Her skin was creamy and clear with a smattering of tiny freckles that perfectly dotted her cheeks and nose in a subtle way. Despite not having braces, her teeth were straight, and her smile—when given—was nice. But looks didn't matter to anyone at camp, so for Beck to call her beautiful seemed irrelevant.

"I'm not your competition. I'm her brother, Hewson Harper," he snapped. "I'm in charge of this camp. And I can tell you right now, Novah's not open for games." He looked at Beck expectantly. "And you are?"

"Open for games," Beck joked, but his words only made Hewson's hard glare narrow even more. "I'm kidding." He reached his hand out. "Beck Haslett."

Hewson eyed the gesture but decided to ignore it. He tugged Novah toward camp, letting her lean on him as she walked over the uneven ground. "Come on. Let's go."

One glance back was all she allowed herself. But it was enough to see Beck's full smile.

Novah

Summer 2059 - Present Day

EVERY FEELING NOVAH had for Beck unleashed inside her. She thought she'd figured out over the last year how to think about him without it completely shattering her heart, and she'd done a good job convincing herself she didn't care—until now.

She pushed her way to the front of the crowd, watching as a caravan of haggard people dragged themselves into camp.

New survivors. Even if Beck didn't make it, the mission would be called a success. He'd brought the most people to camp between the survivors he'd brought with him a year and a half ago and these new ones.

Novah quickly scanned the tired faces for his, but he was nowhere.

Panic ate at her just like poison. What if Beck really hadn't made it back? It would destroy her. This was the exact reason why she'd pushed him away in the first place. She didn't have the strength to love somebody again just to lose them. The world was a rough place—it would eventually swallow up anything she held dear. It was easier to be alone.

The new survivors' footsteps were heavy with fatigue as they collapsed into the open arms of the camp dwellers. Tears of gratitude and relief fell without shame.

Novah wanted to keep looking for Beck, but she had to remind herself that these people mattered more than her own needs and wants. She hugged a stranger tightly, letting the fragile girl weep into her shoulder.

"I never thought we'd make it," the young girl sobbed, clinging to her.

"You're safe now." She ran her hand over the girl's tangled black hair. "You're safe."

Her words felt like empty promises. Was anyone really safe? Life experience had taught her that it was just a matter of time until the catastrophes of the world caught up to people.

"Did you find any animals out there?" Hewson's voice was sharp as he looked over the newcomers. He was never one for sentimental moments, always wanting to get down to business, and animals were a huge asset to their survival.

The crowd split, and Drew moved forward. He looked years older than Novah remembered. Carved into the frail lines of his face were the hardships of the past year. His eyes sunk in, and his cheeks were hollowed out by struggle and hunger.

"We found a cow, but we had to make a decision," Drew said.

"What kind of decision? You know animals are scarce." Hewson threw his hands out, obviously frustrated. "We needed that cow."

"The animal was going lame," Drew stammered,

"and Beck decided the cow would benefit the group more if—"

"Oh, Beck decided." Hewson let out a huff, his irritation growing. "It all makes perfect sense now."

It was like somebody had their hands on two strings inside Novah's stomach and pulled them taut, cinching her anxieties tighter. They hadn't even been here one minute, and Hewson was already mad at Beck. And maybe his anger was all for nothing. Maybe Beck was dead, his body left to decay somewhere along the way.

"Yeah, *I* decided."

Novah's heart lurched into her throat, and she blinked back the rush of emotion that filled her eyes.

Beck.

Her gaze slowly drifted to the familiar sound of his voice.

Beck stepped from behind the crowd. He was taller than Hewson, adding another inch or two with his dirty-blond hair wrapped into a bun on top of his head. A short beard covered his jaw and mouth, adding to his new lumberjack look. Where Drew looked weak and hollow from the journey, Beck looked strong and capable. He looked different from the man she'd remembered a year ago but somehow more handsome, like time had blessed him.

He stared back at her brother, refusing to be intimidated. "It's good to see you, Hewson."

Hewson ignored the salutation. "What exactly did *you* decide to do with the cow?"

"We ate it," Beck replied coolly, dropping his hand.

"How selfish can you be?"

"You weren't out there," Drew said, coming to Beck's defense. "We were dying of hunger, and that cow was the only reason we made it back."

Novah held her breath, waiting for Hewson's response. The tension between them ignited again. The year apart hadn't eased Hewson's hatred.

"Let's hope the loss of that cow isn't the reason an entire population of cows goes extinct." Hewson turned, heading back to camp as he pushed past the crowd.

"Ignore him," Danny said, picking up some of the newcomers' belongings. "We're so glad y'all made it. Let's get everyone some food and rest." The group followed him and his worn-out cowboy hat into camp.

Novah took the shoulder bag from the girl who had been crying in her arms. "Let me carry this for you."

"No, I got it." She glanced down at Novah's foot as if she'd already noticed the limp.

"A personal casualty from the last few years." Novah shrugged.

"I'm sorry," the girl said with a weary smile. She was younger than Novah, probably in her late teens. Her body was petite and malnourished, but she was beautiful with her dark-as-night skin, pink lips, and long lashes.

"Don't be." Novah straightened, leaning on her fake acceptance of the injury. "Everyone's lost something."

"I'm Indonesia," the girl said. Novah looked at her, perplexed, wondering why in the world her mother would name her something like that. She must've been used to the look on Novah's face because she quickly added, "I was born the day Mt. Toba erupted in Indonesia." She raised her tiny shoulders. "My mother had a weird sense of humor."

"You were born on August 3rd, 2041?" That date was burned into Novah's memory—probably burned into every survivor's mind the way significant dates in history were.

"Yep." Indonesia put a lock of black hair behind her ear. "Pretty crazy birthday, huh?"

The eruption of the supervolcano was the beginning of the end. It triggered the start of a worldwide destruction that had lasted for nineteen years—*Desolation*, as the survivors called it. Novah was only five when the volcano erupted and was oblivious to what was happening in the world, but as she'd grown up dealing with the repercussions of that day, the date had stayed with her.

"It's nice to meet you, Indonesia."

"Oh, everyone calls me Indie. It's much easier."

Novah nodded, slinging her arm around the young girl's shoulder as if she was somehow going to help *her* to camp. But just as they took a few steps forward, Beck stopped in the middle of the path, blocking their way.

It wasn't just his broad shoulders and chest that felt intimidating. It was the way Novah's body reacted to his nearness. Something dangerous and addictive fluttered in her heart. She felt his gaze on her, the way it always had been, so she glanced up.

That was a mistake.

Beck's stare was full of questions that Novah couldn't answer. But behind all the questions, his gaze held deep-rooted passion, causing a desolation-esque fire to run rampant in her chest.

"It's good to see you, Novah." His deep voice rumbled through her body, vibrating every nerve. But the best part of seeing him again was Beck's smile. It was genuine, like he'd thought about her every day for the last year.

She hadn't missed a day thinking about him, but she'd never admit that, especially to Beck. He was the type of guy that needed little to no encouragement to have hope, and hope was the last thing anyone at camp should ever have. Their relationship couldn't fall back to where they'd started a year and a half ago when he'd first come. Too much had passed between them that couldn't be undone.

She looked down, pretending to focus on her footsteps. "I'm glad *you all* made it back safely." It was better to make her words about the group, not Beck specifically.

Was she glad he was back?

Her mind said no—Beck's arrival complicated everything—but her heart screamed yes. Sometimes it was hard to know which part of herself knew her best.

Her shoulder brushed his arm as she walked past with Indie. Beck gently grabbed her elbow, pausing her footsteps and the breath in her lungs as a slow trickle of chills traveled down her body.

It had been a year.

How could his touch do so much damage one year later? Hadn't she spent every day building back up the wall around her heart? Hadn't she rehearsed all the reasons why they couldn't be together? Hadn't she chosen Hewson over him?

But standing there, with his rough fingers on her elbow and her heart trembling, Novah knew her efforts had been a waste. She'd never be released from her feelings for Beck Haslett.

He bent down, placing his lips close to her ear. Novah stiffened, holding still, as if she were a statue that felt nothing. "You're all I've thought about for an entire year."

Beck's words weren't filled with his signature flirtatiousness. The tone was sincere and honest. The warm whispers melted the edges of her frozen-solid heart, and she shivered as his lips grazed the side of her ear. Novah ached for him more than she ever had, but she swallowed hard, slowly slinking out of his grasp. She needed to get control.

"Come on, Indie. Let's get you settled."

But nothing about her felt settled. She walked away, her insides rattling everywhere, and Beck was the one who shook them up.

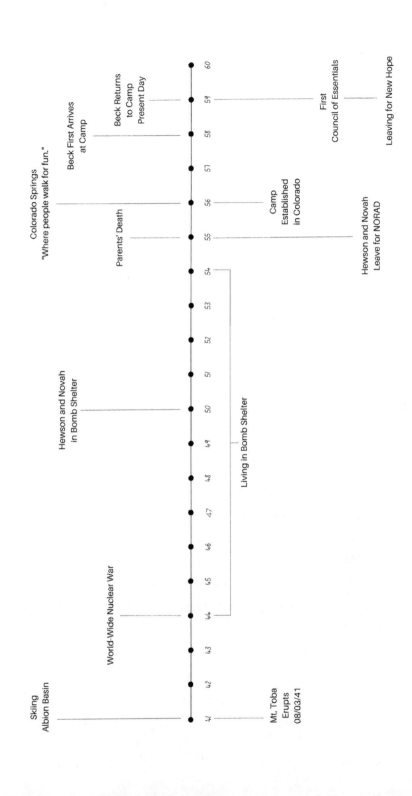

2

Novah

Spring 2058 - A Year and a Half Ago

Novah walked downstream to a place where she could be alone. The newcomers that had arrived yesterday were a disappointing reminder that her parents were dead. It conjured up familiar *why are those people still alive and my parents aren't?* questions. But deep down, Novah knew the answer. It was *her* fault that her parents were taken from her, and that was why the ache in her chest throbbed uncomfortably day in and day out.

She sat down on a boulder by the river and removed her socks and shoes, easing her swollen foot into the water. The cold liquid helped with the pain and swelling on days when her ankle hurt more than usual. Today was one of those days.

A bird chirped far up in a tree, competing with the sound of the river. She sucked in a breath and felt the dampness of the earth deep inside her lungs. She leaned back against her hands and raised her chin, closing her eyes as the water rushed around her ankles. The moment was peaceful, which felt odd because nothing inside her held *peace*.

Not anymore.

"I feel like I'm interrupting."

Novah's eyes flew open, and her neck craned to see behind her.

"But I also feel like it would be weird if I just left." Beck stood a few feet away, hands casually in his pockets. His dusty-blond hair was still doing that attractive thing where one piece hung perfectly over his forehead like a weapon meant to lure women in. Then, there was his smile filled with true happiness. What was so great about Beck's life that made him smile like that?

It was annoying how good-looking he was, but even more annoying was how alert Novah had been since he'd arrived in camp the day before. Not the good kind of alert, where you're focused on staying alive. No, Novah's nerves were on edge, like they knew exactly where Beck was at all times, anticipating his nearness, hoping for it. She'd even spent extra time readying herself for the day. He'd called her beautiful, and for some reason, she wanted to live up to that label.

She blinked at him standing there, unsure what to say. She had little to no practice talking to a man as attractive as him.

"I mean, you're enjoying the river so much that I've got to try it too, don't I?"

Something about them there together—*alone*—made Novah nervous. She scooted forward. "I was just about to leave."

"No, you weren't." Beck laughed.

He kicked off his shoes and then bent down to remove his socks. He was obviously planning on sitting with her. There was no point in pretending like she was leaving. She'd have to face the uneasy feeling head-on. Beck hopped over a few boulders until he got to the one she was on and sat down, his shoulder brushing against hers.

"Novah Harper, right?"

"You remember." She looked straight ahead because meeting his gaze seemed too intimate, especially considering how close they were sitting to each other.

"We only met yesterday, so it wasn't too hard to remember."

"You've probably met a hundred people since then."

"But nobody as pretty as you."

All the extra time she'd spent on her hair that morning suddenly felt worth it.

Novah's curiosity was piqued, and she turned her head. Beck's charming smile was aimed right at her. The butterflies slowly drifting through her stomach were a direct contradiction to everything she'd felt as an adult— a misplaced emotion that felt foreign. Is this what it felt like to be hit on? She was twenty-three and, because of

Desolation, had never experienced anything like this. Sure, there were a few men around camp that had smiled at her, but they mostly kept their distance.

She chose a hesitant smile in response. "I see you're fluent in bull crap."

His eyebrows raised a tad, adding a playfulness to his words. "And I see you're fluent in cynicism."

"After everything we've been through during Desolation, aren't we all?"

"Eh, I don't know. Things aren't that bad." Beck leaned back and rested his weight against his hands, kicking his legs out in front of him. He looked so carefree and relaxed that Novah blinked just to make sure she wasn't dreaming him up.

"Not that bad!" she scoffed. "Let me ask you a question." She leaned forward. "When was the last time you've been full?"

"Like with food?"

"Yeah. You know, completely satisfied and stuffed. You couldn't eat anything else even if you wanted to."

His eyes squinted together as he looked off into the distance. "I'd say June 12th, 2044."

"That was fourteen years ago. I think that's proof enough that we have it bad." Novah relaxed into her position on the rock, satisfied that her point had been made. But that was when more curiosity set in, and she flipped her eyes to him. "What happened June 12th, 2044?"

"I have no clue." His smile widened as if he'd just

gotten braces off and wanted everyone to see his straight teeth. "I just made that date up for the sake of the conversation."

"Ugh." Novah rolled her eyes. "Are you always this happy?"

"You can't *always* be something, but yeah. I like to think of myself as a pretty positive guy."

"Well, you and I aren't going to get along, then."

"Don't write us off just yet." His flirty smile was back. "I think we could become great friends."

Novah lifted her chin as a sign—if just to herself—that Beck's charms couldn't win her over. "I'm not sure why you think that. You don't know anything about me."

"Let's change that." He pointed to her foot. "What happened?"

She bit her lip, glancing away from his probing stare.

"Oh." Beck leaned forward to meet her eyes. "Are we supposed to pretend that you don't have a bad foot?"

"No." Her brows furrowed at the same time her glare shot to him.

"Then, what happened?"

Novah didn't talk about herself or her past. She brushed it all aside, as if everything that had happened didn't matter. It was easier to live in a pretend world than to face the pain straight on.

"Well?" Beck pressed.

Her tongue brimmed with the answer, and for some reason, she didn't hold it in.

"My foot got trapped between debris during a

tornado, and my ankle fractured. Without a doctor to set it properly, it could never heal the correct way. So, now I get to deal with the pain and swelling." She searched Beck's face for the sympathy stare she was accustomed to seeing from people—the look that said they pitied her and counted her out—but with Beck, it wasn't there.

He shrugged. "Well, at least you didn't lose it completely. It's great you can still walk on it."

Novah's eyes narrowed. Everyone knew that someone maimed or injured was a liability that others had to make up for and carry their weight. Nothing about her situation was *great*.

"What?" He lifted his brows as he studied her skeptical expression. "I'm sure it's painful, and it sucks, and it slows you down, but you can still get around. That's the important thing, right? You're probably grateful."

A small spurt of laughter rolled over her lips. "I wouldn't say I'm *grateful* for the injury."

"Well, *you* wouldn't." Playful eyes matched his joking smile. "As we noted earlier, you speak fluent cynicism. And that's exactly why we should be friends. I'll help you find happiness in bad situations."

"That sounds annoying." Novah's lips twitched, but she held her mouth steady, not ready to reveal her smile.

"It depends on how you look at it."

"I'm looking at it like it's annoying."

Beck's grin widened. "That's not a real argument."

"Yes, it is." She straightened.

"No, it's not. You don't have a leg to stand on, so you better get used to being my friend."

"I don't have a leg to stand on?" Novah frowned, but Beck's smile stayed firm on his face, poking at her walls until she finally spoke. "That's funny," she said matter-of-factly, then she tilted her head, thinking it over some more. A slow smile spread across her lips. "Actually, that's really funny."

"See?" His chest puffed out. "You're already glad that we're friends."

"I wouldn't go that far." She tucked her smile back in. "Besides, why would someone like you want to be friends with me anyway? Shouldn't you surround yourself with other people who love to be happy?"

"Where's the satisfaction in that?" The green in Beck's hazel eyes lit up. "It's so much more rewarding when you finally get a smile from someone who doesn't give them away easily."

"So, I'm like a project to you? Let's cheer up the crippled girl?"

"Do you need cheering up?" There was a sharpness behind his stare that made Novah feel like he could see through her skin to her soul.

She hugged her arms around her body, trying to block his view of her deepest secrets, and glanced away. "I'm sure if you asked anyone at camp, they'd say that I need cheering up."

It's not like she wasn't friendly, but she certainly wasn't the life of the party.

"I'm not so sure about that." He leaned back against his hands again, resuming his relaxed position. "From what I've seen, the people at camp would say you're kind-hearted and giving."

Novah shifted in her seat, uncomfortable with the direction the conversation was taking. "You've been here a day and a half. What could you have possibly seen?"

"I saw you playing tic-tac-toe in the dirt with a few kids."

Novah rolled her eyes. "That was nothing."

"What about when you gave half of your dinner to that old lady last night?"

He saw that?

Novah had waited until nobody was around to trade Yasmin plates.

"No wonder you're never full." There was a sarcastic tilt to Beck's mouth that made Novah bite back her smile.

"Well, she's dying." Novah turned her head away. "She should at least be allowed to have some mediocre squash before her life ends."

"And what about the time you spent cutting all the newcomers' hair yesterday? You were on your feet for hours." His eyes darted to her ankle. "Which I'm sure is why you're in so much pain today. But you never complained."

"If this is your attempt to make me want to be friends with you, it's backfiring. I'm leaving this conversation freaked out by how much you've been watching me. I'll probably need to get a restraining order against you."

Her father had been a lawyer and had taught her all about that kind of stuff, but that was years ago.

Beck laughed good-naturedly. "Can't come within fifty yards of you."

She liked that he knew what she was talking about.

"More like one hundred yards." A small smirk hinted that she wasn't actually alarmed by his stalker ways. If Novah was being honest, she was flattered.

"Good thing I brought binoculars with me. One hundred yards is totally still doable."

Novah couldn't help it.

She laughed.

It sounded weird coming from her, but she didn't stop herself.

Beck watched her with a joyous smile that could summon a choir of angels to sing behind him. "I like your laugh. You should do it more."

She rolled her lips together. Her eyes met his, and her stomach turned over. "There hasn't been anything to laugh about."

"I'd like to change that."

They held each other's stare for a second—something that Novah would normally think was awkward, but with Beck, it was exciting.

But that was when the alarms went off inside her.

Maybe in the old world, before Desolation, a woman could get excited about a man hitting on her. But not now. Love and relationships were a frivolous luxury of the past. These days, relationships were about how that person could help you survive. What could they offer that would increase your chance of making it out of this nightmare?

"Listen, I'll save you the time and energy." Novah shifted her eyes to the moving water. "I'm not interested in friendship or anything *more* than friendship. It's just my brother and me, and that's how I prefer it."

"Your brother." Beck whistled. "He seems super… *nice.*" Novah didn't miss the sarcasm in his voice.

"Hewson has the weight of the world on his shoulders," she defended. "He's pretty much the leader of the entire camp."

"I can't imagine why."

She narrowed her eyes.

"I'm kidding. I'm sure he's very capable. But being a leader doesn't mean you have the right to treat everyone like crap." For the first time in their conversation, his eyes turned serious. "A good leader builds people up, unifies, and gives hope."

Hope.

Novah couldn't remember the last time she'd had hope—but for a second there, with Beck, maybe she had a glimpse of it. That was exactly why being with him was so dangerous.

"But okay, if you say we can't be friends, then I'll respect that." Beck suddenly hopped to his feet. "I'll leave you alone now."

She looked at him, confused and a little disappointed.

Was he really going to give up that easily? Would it have been so terrible if he put up a little resistance?

"That's it?" she asked.

"I'm leaving you wanting more so that maybe you'll change your mind about us." He smiled down at her. "At least that's what I hope I'm doing." He grabbed his shoes and socks and started to walk away, turning over his shoulder with a wide smile. "I'll see you around, Novah Harper." Then, Beck disappeared between the trees.

Novah swirled her foot in the water below. That was the strangest ten minutes she'd ever had with a man. They didn't talk about anything substantial, make any plans about survival, or trade any goods. It was all just fluff, but somehow, that fluff had left her feeling lighter. Despite the red flags waving in her mind, she wanted that lightness back.

Beck had been successful. He'd left her wanting more.

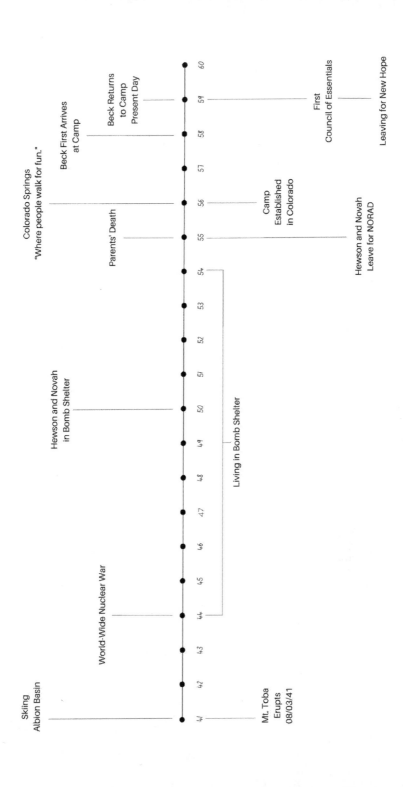

3

Beck

Summer 2059 - Present Day

"So, we come upon this clothing store that was mostly still intact," Beck explained to a group of people sitting in a circle that night after dinner. The orange glow of flames from the fire lit his face as he spoke.

He'd always liked telling his younger sisters ghost stories around a campfire. This story was more humorous than *ghost*, but it felt good to do something that reminded him of the time before the world fell apart.

"And I think to myself, we need to gather up as many clothes as we can carry. So, I told Drew to wait with the group while I checked it out. I climbed over the rubble and made my way into the storefront just to find out it was a women's lingerie store." Laughter bubbled out from his listeners, urging him to continue. "I couldn't really be disappointed. I mean, who doesn't love lingerie?" More giggles from around the fire.

"I don't buy that," Hewson muttered across the circle.

"You don't buy lingerie?" Beck's brows lifted in a teasing way. "That's really a shame." He shouldn't joke with Hewson. It never ended well.

"No." Hewson ignored the snickers around him. "I don't buy that you weren't disappointed. Real clothes could mean a lot to our survival."

"Oh, these were real." Beck raised the corner of his mouth. "Silky and soft."

Hewson didn't find it amusing.

"Beck left out the best part." Drew chuckled, taking it upon himself to finish the story. "He came out from the store *wearing* the lingerie." He paused, trying to catch his breath between laughs. "He wore a lacey, red bra and panties under a see-through nighty. And on his head, a black thong."

An older woman shouted over the laughter. "Please tell me he had his regular clothes on under."

"Just his underwear!" Drew burst out.

Beck shook his head, trying to conceal his smile. "Don't believe a word Drew says. I would never do something like that."

"Yes, you would. And you *did,*" Stephanie, an older woman from the rescue party, chimed in. "We weren't complaining. He looked good, even with panties on over his boxers."

"Thanks, Steph." Beck smiled. "I'm very popular with women ages sixty-five and older."

More laughter.

Beck shrugged. "Eh, it had been a rough couple of days of travel, and I was just trying to put a smile on everyone's face. You know, keep morale up."

"You did." Stephanie's weary eyes stared at him from the other side of the circle. "That little lingerie stunt of yours filled me up enough to keep going a few more days." She blew a motherly kiss to him. "None of us would be here if it wasn't for you. You're our savior and the best man I know."

He appreciated her kind words. He just wished *everyone* felt the same as Stephanie.

Beck glanced at Novah. He loved watching her when she didn't know he was looking. Tonight, she sat next to Hewson like she always did, holding back her smile, probably not sure if she should laugh at his story when her brother was around. She stared absently into the fire, giving Beck another chance to rove his eyes over her. Her brown hair was longer and highlighted in the front from the summer sun. A long braid flipped over her shoulder on one side. She wore the same red and blue flannel shirt, buttons undone, with the same oversized gray t-shirt that said *Moody Family Reunion 2039*. Her faded jeans hung loose on her, and her knees poked through large holes. His lips lifted as he studied her. Everything about her was more beautiful than he'd remembered.

Beck had recreated, in his mind, each of her features

every night when he closed his eyes. But even the last year of remembering her hadn't done her beauty justice. Novah was better in person than anything his mind had ever conjured up.

He'd missed looking at her soft face and big brown eyes. But it was more than that. He'd missed *her.* He missed how she smiled when he told a joke, as if it was the first time in her life that anyone had said something funny. He missed her opinions, even though it took some prodding to get her to express them. He missed the look in her eyes when she talked about happy memories from her childhood. And he missed her quiet strength. Novah didn't know she was strong, but Beck did.

While he was gone, she had tormented his thoughts. He thought he'd gotten to a point where he could let her go and move on with his life. But as the year stretched on, and as they got closer to camp, his heart had convinced his head to try one last time. He was back, and he didn't want Novah to be just a thought. He wanted her to be a real part of his life. She was worth the extra effort and the heartache that might come with it.

"The truth is"—Beck kept his eyes on Novah—"I carried a whole bunch of stuff with us from that lingerie store." He waited until she met his gaze. It didn't take long for her brown eyes to peek up at him. "I've got a lot of stuff that would look good on you"—he paused before adding—"*women.*"

Hewson scoffed next to her, but she avoided his heated glare, looking down at the ground instead.

"And all joking aside," Stephanie said, "new underwear is nice to have."

"How did you carry it all that way?" Hewson asked with an annoyance that couldn't be missed.

"We carried a lot of stuff in the wagon. Seeds, salvaged items, anything we could find that we thought would be useful," Drew explained.

"We can go through all the stuff in your wagon tomorrow." Hewson stood. "I think we should get some rest for the night." He looked around at some of the newcomers. "We sleep in the caves. Find yourself an open spot."

Everyone took Hewson's cue that it was bedtime. It was obvious he still thought he was in charge of the camps. That much hadn't changed. In the morning, he'd probably want to show the newcomers around the two other camps along the bench of the mountain. He'd take the entire group like they were on some kind of museum tour, showing them the other six-thousand survivors spread out in camps two and three. He'd tell them everything *he* built and organized. Anything to stroke his ego.

Novah stood next to Hewson, waiting for him to finish a conversation with another man. Beck hated how everything in her life was dependent on her brother. He controlled everything she did, and for some reason, Novah let him. But this time, Beck promised himself he wouldn't let Hewson get in the way of their relationship. He'd keep a wide berth when it came to Hewson Harper.

Because loving Novah meant not getting into fights with her brother.

She peeked at Beck while she waited. He smiled, noting how she bit her bottom lip nervously. Did she want to talk to him as much as he wanted to talk to her? He hoped. But earlier today, when they'd first arrived in camp, she had the chance to say more and didn't take it. Her guard was up, but breaking it down again just became Beck's number one goal.

He'd done it once before.

Surely, he could do it again.

4

Beck

Spring 2058 - A Year and a Half Ago

Beck sat on a stump in the shade of a large boulder, sharpening the blade of his Swiss Army knife. It was one of the few possessions that he'd kept with him from before Desolation—a present from his father on his eleventh birthday. He felt lazy here but in a good way. He hadn't had a consistent home for more than five years. He'd constantly been on the move, helping survivors he'd found along the way.

But now, things were different. His day wasn't about finding people or getting to a destination. Now, it was about building a future. He'd thought about the future for almost a decade—what his life would look like when he finally came out from under the storm of life. He never imagined he'd be sitting on the benches of the Cheyenne Mountains, but he welcomed the change of pace, especially since his new home came with an intriguing, beautiful woman.

Novah Harper.

She was a mystery to Beck, a puzzle he wanted to spend hours poring over just to put the last piece in place so he could see the full picture. Right now, all he saw was the halo of sadness and self-doubt that hung around her —feelings he intended to dismantle. But there was more to her than that. Beck just needed time to peel back all the layers.

His eyes swung to where she stood twenty feet away on a tree stump by the cave's opening. Beck didn't know what exactly she was doing, but it looked like she was measuring something, then she'd step off and kneel down in front of pieces of fabric she'd laid out. She stood again, making her way to the stump by the cave. Her gaze darted to him as if she could feel his eyes on her. Beck smirked, dropping his head so his focus was on his blade again. He should've been done sharpening his knife by now, but Novah was a good distraction that kept him there.

Hewson came up the hill, carrying a stack of vegetables from the field. He caught the last seconds of Novah hopping off the tree stump.

"What are you doing?"

"Nothing." She straightened.

He dropped the vegetables to the ground by the washbin. "You're going to hurt yourself."

"I'm fine." She shook her head, walking back to the pieces of fabric spread out on the ground.

Hewson pointed to where she worked. "What's all this?"

"I'm making something we can drape across the opening of the cave when the weather is bad. You know, to keep a little bit of the heat in."

He placed his hands on his hips. "Don't be stupid. You can't handle that."

She gave her brother a pointed stare. "It's just a bad foot. I can still do things."

Hewson wrapped his arm around her waist, escorting her to the couch in front of the fire. "No, you can't. The last thing I need is for you to reinjure your ankle and not be able to walk at all. I don't have time to deal with that."

Beck's jaw tightened as he listened to how her brother treated her. At least he knew now where all her self-doubts came from.

"I was just trying to be helpful." Novah eased down onto the couch.

"What's helpful is if you just listen to me and stay out of trouble," Hewson muttered, turning his back to her. "I think we've learned from experience that it's best if you just stay put. I'll go get your bag so you have something to do."

Novah's eyes fell to her hands, and she didn't say anything more. Why didn't she stand up to her brother? Beck had seen her backbone down by the river two days ago when she'd told him she didn't want to be friends.

Why didn't she use some of that same spunk against her brother?

What did Hewson have over her?

Novah

NOVAH FUMED, tapping her pencil on the blank page in front of her. She hated feeling helpless. She wanted to contribute around camp, but Hewson constantly counted her out, and the worst part was that he was right. She couldn't afford to reinjure her ankle again. Thanks to her own stupidity, she'd already done that once. She didn't need another reason for Hewson to resent her.

The afternoon sun was hidden by clouds, cooling the temperature to something a little more comfortable. She looked down at her notebook. The blank lines judged her for not writing an entry yet for this year. When Novah lived in the bomb shelter with her family, she wrote in her notebook all the time. It was something that her mother had encouraged her to do to cope with being caged in. Her mother credited her own journal entries to saving her insanity, but now that Novah was older, she knew it was the bottle of anxiety pills that had saved her mother during those years. Novah wished she'd taken the Xanax bottle with them when they left the shelter instead of leaving the pills behind to rot. She could really use a dose of something calming in her life right now.

"Hey, there." The springs on the couch popped as Beck sat down on the other end.

She'd seen him watching her earlier and hoped he hadn't heard Hewson chastise her for trying to work.

She flipped her head to him. "Do you make it a habit of interrupting people when they clearly want to be alone?" She instantly regretted how sharp her words came out. She was mad at Hewson, not Beck.

But he just smiled. "How am I supposed to know if you want to be alone or not?"

Novah's lips twitched, grateful he'd brushed off her harsh words. "The fact that I'm sitting alone should've been a dead giveaway."

"Nah, I assumed you're always sitting alone because you don't have any friends. You just keep pushing people away."

"Maybe because I like being alone."

Except, right now, being alone was the last thing she wanted. She'd been thinking about Beck ever since their conversation by the river two days ago, when he'd barged into her life with cheeriness, asking all kinds of personal questions. He was the exact opposite of what she thought she'd like, but since then, Novah had been brainstorming how Beck could add to her survival. What could she trade him just to be able to spend a little more time with him? How could a friendship with him benefit her? Because that was how it worked in Desolation. The value of a person was in what you gained from them or how they helped you.

"Well, you're not alone anymore, so get over it." He

smiled as he said the words, contradicting his bossiness. He glanced at her paper. "What are you working on?"

There was no way she was going to tell him that she needed to write in her diary but she couldn't come up with anything to say because everything about her life was miserable. So, she said what she thought he wanted to hear.

"Nothing, really." She gestured to her pink glitter backpack leaning against the arm of the couch. "Just going through some of my old stuff I brought with me from Kansas." She flipped through the pages of her notebook.

"Is that a picture of Zan Hughes? With a heart around it?" Beck leaned forward, trying to get a better look.

Novah quickly closed her notebook, feeling embarrassed. "No."

"Yes, I believe it was." He grabbed the book out of her hands.

"Beck!" she squealed, reaching to get it back, but he was already flipping through the pages until he found the one with the magazine cutout of Zan Hughes glued to it.

"Oh my goodness!" He smiled. "It is Zan Hughes. I used to make fun of his YouTube channel when I was young."

"Well, he got the last laugh because he became a real actor."

He shook his head. "I can't believe you have a crush on Zan Hughes."

Her face flushed. "*Had.* Had a crush on Zan Hughes."

"This was more than a crush." Beck examined the page full of drawn hearts and cursive signatures of *Novah Harper Hughes*. "This was true love."

She rolled her eyes. "True love at ten years old. I doubt it."

"You carried it with you all these years. That must mean something."

"I carried it with me because paper and pens are hard to come by now."

"I think you carried it all these years to give you hope." Beck smiled, wagging his eyebrows. "Hope for love in the future."

"Give me a break," Novah scoffed. "Do I seem like the kind of girl who hopes for love?"

Beck's eyes turned serious, and his playful smile faded. "No, you seem like the type of girl who's been through a lot and doesn't know where to go from here."

Was he playing pin the tail on the donkey? Or pin the emotions on the broken girl? Whatever Beck's game, he just hit it right on the target.

He handed the notebook back, his eyes never leaving hers. "But I'm glad you still have things like this to remind you of happier times. Something that special needs to be taken care of."

A flood of feelings ripped through her chest. She couldn't decide if she liked them or if they were eating her alive.

"Not anymore." She ripped the paper out, crumpling it up and throwing it into the fire pit.

Beck's eyes followed the crumpled ball as it sailed into the pit, landing in a pile of ashes on the edge of the dried-up wood. "Why did you do that?"

"The past is gone. There's no point in reliving it."

"I see." He nodded to the field below, where Hewson went to gather more vegetables. "What about your brother? Does he feel the same way about the past?"

No.

Hewson loved to throw the past in her face whenever it suited him.

"Of course." She lifted her chin. "We're all about moving on."

"I see." Nothing about Beck's expression made her think he believed a word she'd said.

"What's the deal with you and your brother anyway? He seems a little overbearing."

"He has to be. We're all we have left."

"If you're all each other has left, you'd think he'd be a little kinder to you. Take care of you better."

"Hewson takes care of me just fine," she snapped. "I owe everything to him."

"Okay." He held up his hands in a gesture of peace. "I was just trying to understand your relationship, but I see this is a sensitive subject."

Novah stood and packed up her things. "It's not a sensitive subject, and I don't need you to understand our relationship."

She understood it plenty well herself.

"I'm going to go start prepping for dinner." She walked away before Beck saw the tears threatening her eyes.

What was this man doing to her? She barely knew the guy, and yet, somehow, he stirred up things in her that she'd tried to push aside.

And the weirdest part was that she wasn't even mad at him for it.

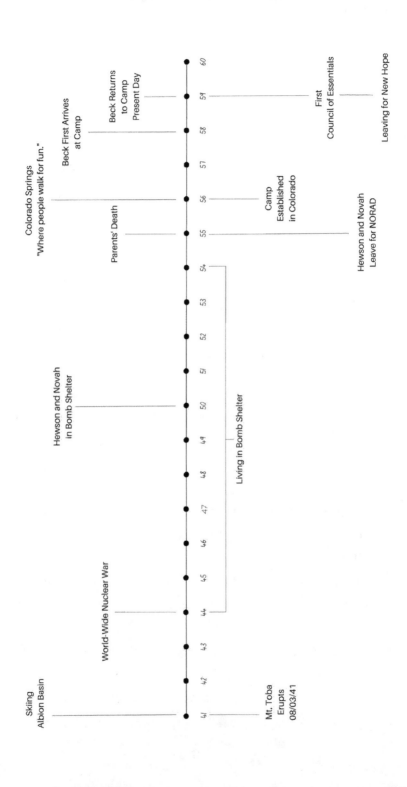

Skiing
Albion Basin

World-Wide Nuclear War

Hewson and Novah
in Bomb Shelter

Colorado Springs
"Where people walk for fun."

Beck First Arrives
at Camp

Beck Returns
to Camp
Present Day

Parents' Death

Mt. Toba
Erupts
08/03/41

Living in Bomb Shelter

Camp
Established
in Colorado

Hewson and Novah
Leave for NORAD

First
Council of Essentials

Leaving for New Hope

41 42 43 44 45 46 47 48 49 50 51 52 53 54 55 56 57 58 59 60

5

Hewson

February 2044 - Fifteen Years Ago

"Hewson, turn the TV up!" His mother flipped her hand toward the flat screen, covering her mouth with her other hand as they watched the replay of an atomic bomb hitting the city of St. Louis.

CNN played the cell phone footage of a flood of light so bright Hewson thought the sun had blown up. Then, an orange fireball was gurgled up in the flames and darkened into a purple-hued column of smoke.

"Another atomic bomb?" Hewson tried to read the moving words at the bottom of the screen, but they were moving too fast.

"Shh!" his mother cried, straining to hear the TV over his father's loud voice on the phone in the kitchen.

A news reporter's words played over the videos. "February 7, 2044: North Korea, Japan, and China drop another atomic bomb on the United States. This is the second bomb in the US in four days and the fifth atomic bomb hitting this side of the hemisphere this week. Other bombs struck New York, Toronto, Sao Paulo, and Buenos Aires."

"Two bombs in the US in one week." Hewson watched the news flip over to the nuclear aftermath in Manhattan. The news reporter wore a gas mask and protective gear, pointing behind him as the camera zoomed in on the new ground zero. Hewson was only fourteen but had learned about Hiroshima and Nagasaki in school. He knew about the devastating results of bombs of this caliber.

"Madison?" His dad rushed into the room, cell phone in hand. He looked directly at his mom. "Mike Wilson has a bomb shelter in northern Wisconsin that we can stay in." His dad combed his fingers through his hair, a panicked expression filling his eyes. "I mean, we all thought he was crazy when he built it two years ago, but he was right."

"Why Wisconsin?" his mother asked.

"Years ago, his dad was one of the lawyers for the Green Bay Packers, and his family still has some land there. So, I think we should go."

"Christian, we can't..." His mother's words trailed off.

He gave a defeated shrug. "We'd need to pack now."

"Now?" Hewson's mother looked at Novah playing

Barbies on the floor in front of the TV, oblivious to the attacks.

"Yes. Mike's only letting a few families come. We need to make sure we're one of them."

Hewson wanted to believe that they were safe. A bomb shelter? That had to be an overreaction. "Dad, nobody will drop a nuclear bomb on Kansas. It's *Kansas*."

"We don't know that. There have already been two bombs this week." His father's brows dropped in agitation. "I have to protect our family."

"The US will strike back!" Hewson had all the naiveté of a fourteen-year-old boy. "We'll show the world who's in charge."

"I'm sure the United States will strike back, but it doesn't matter. What's done is done. Hundreds of thousands of people have lost their lives. All because our country couldn't share food and resources. Since the eruption, people have been starving in Asia because of the volcanic winter. Disease swept through the continent, and the US won't let anyone from those countries in. They're desperate over there, and our country ignored their pleas for help." He pointed to the TV. "This is the consequence." His body shifted as his eyes darted across the room to Hewson's mom. "Madison, I think we should do this." His mother's brown eyes filled with moisture, causing his father to walk to her. He sat down on the couch and grabbed her hands. "Am I overreacting? Please tell me if I'm overreacting." He sucked in a deep breath. "I just need to keep you and Hewson and Novah safe…at all costs."

"I know. I just can't believe we're at this place, making these kinds of decisions." A tear dripped down her face. "If you feel like this is the right thing to do, then let's go. If it's an overreaction, we can always come back in a few weeks. No harm done."

"Okay, I'll let Mike know we're coming." His father stood. "Pack only the things we absolutely need." He rushed into the kitchen, then popped his head out to add, "Food. We need food and water. If a bomb hits the Wisconsin area, there won't be food for a long time. And a generator! And flashlights, batteries, and first aid. Medications!" He shouted out survival items as if they were popping into his head like a group text thread gone wild.

All of the color drained from his mom's face. She moved slowly, just going through the motions, not really concentrating on anything real.

"Mommy?" Novah's tiny voice asked.

"Yes, baby?" Hewson was surprised that his mom could muster a fake smile for Novah.

"Can I bring my Barbies on our vacation?"

Vacation?

Hewson wanted to believe that this wasn't permanent, that in a few weeks or months, they'd be back in their home in Kansas.

"Of course, you can bring your Barbies."

"And Monopoly?"

"Yes, whatever games you want." She patted Novah's head before walking numbly to her bedroom.

Hewson felt a twinge of panic, but he dutifully stood, heading to the closet where they kept their suitcases.

Hewson

Summer 2059 - Present Day

"WHAT'S IT LIKE OUT THERE?" Hewson asked Drew as they carried supplies from the wagon back to camp. Even though it was still morning, Hewson felt the summer heat getting stronger. A drip of sweat trickled down the center of his back, dampening his t-shirt. "Where can we send people to rebuild?"

"I don't know." Drew released a deep sigh. "There's nothing but crumpled buildings and charred land. Nothing grows there, and nothing is recognizable. As we moved farther inland, I knew we were near St. Louis, but I couldn't see anything in the distance that looked like the Gateway Arch. The atomic bomb ruined everything."

Hewson had already suspected that the land was charred and ruined. He'd known that since he was four-teen. He could still remember watching the news of the bombings on TV.

He shook his head and pushed the memory out of his mind, turning his attention back to Drew. "So, you're saying we can't send a group of people to inhabit that area?"

"Not right where the bombs hit. We don't want to worry about radiation, but the surrounding land might work. It's just a matter of if we want to take that chance or not."

Radiation was a huge concern.

"And the Great Lakes are so much bigger now with the rising water," Drew continued. "I doubt Michigan and Wisconsin even exist anymore."

St. Louis, Chicago, New York City, and Los Angeles were all hit by atomic bombs during the two years the nuclear war took place, but most of those areas were underwater now, taken by tsunamis and the rising water level from advanced global warming, swallowed up into the ocean, never to return again. St. Louis was the only area hit that they could potentially inhabit. But with the changing water table the last few years, so many places had turned into marshland that they'd never be able to grow food and vegetation properly.

Hewson's mind drifted to the bomb shelter he'd spent ten years living in with his family. It was hard to imagine that it might be underwater now.

"Beck thinks the East Coast starts about halfway into North Carolina and all those eastern states."

Beck thinks.

"How could Beck even know that?" Hewson didn't try to hide his annoyance.

"He's from North Carolina. I think he has a good grasp on that area."

Hewson placed his supplies on the ground next to Drew's. "I wouldn't have minded if Beck had never returned to camp." He looked across the field to Beck, who was handing out underwear that he'd collected from the lingerie store. The women around him were all laughing as they held up different sizes and types.

It was starting again.

"Is that rivalry between you two still a thing?" Drew followed his stare to where Beck was standing. "Hasn't it been long enough that you can get over it?"

"It's more than a rivalry. I hate him. But I can get over it if he stays away from me while we figure out the rebuild." Hewson folded his arms. "And stays away from my sister."

"But can your sister stay away from him?" Drew chuckled as he watched Beck hold up a thong and throw it at an older woman, eliciting a laugh from everyone around him. "He's a really likable guy."

Yeah, that was one of the main reasons Hewson didn't like him. Beck's rising popularity was a direct threat to his own role in the future. It was the same thing a year ago, before he'd left. All anyone wanted to talk about back then was what a good leader Beck was. He remembered overhearing a group of people discussing that if they had to vote right then for a president or some kind of leader, they'd vote for Beck. That was three weeks after he'd arrived at camp the first time. The last thing Hewson wanted was for Beck's popularity to gain momentum again. Hewson had built this place through his own sweat and blood. *He* was the one that should be the leader.

But more than that, Beck had tried to turn Novah against him, filling her head with all sorts of lies and ideas. Hopefully, she was smarter now and wouldn't fall for his tricks.

"Novah won't get mixed up with him again." Hewson set his jaw as if he could will his words to be true with his own stubbornness. "She's already made her decision. Besides, we have a lot going on now with planning the rebuild. There's no time for romance."

"I thought we were going to wait until Beck and I got back with the last of the survivors before we would start planning the rebuild, giving us more time to grow crops and gather provisions to survive a rebuild."

Hewson kicked at the dirt. "The longer you were gone, the more we weren't sure if you were ever coming back."

"We were only gone one year."

"Yeah, well, everybody was anxious to start planning the future—to have some certainty in their lives. The crops are growing well. It just seemed like a good time. We couldn't wait any longer."

"More like *you* were anxious to start planning the future."

"I don't know what you're so upset about. We can't

wait around forever or live off this mountain forever. Things have to change."

Drew scoffed. "So, are you telling me you've planned everything already?"

"What's going on over here?" Beck asked, walking up to the conversation. He must've run out of underwear to pass out.

Great. Just what I need.

Drew placed his hands on his hips. "Hewson was just explaining why they moved forward with planning the rebuild without us."

Beck's brows furrowed in confusion.

"Nothing has been decided yet," Hewson hedged. "Each of the three camps nominated two people to represent them. Six people were chosen and are in the beginning stages of making decisions."

"Let me guess. You were nominated from our camp." Beck's laser-sharp eyes landed on Hewson.

"Obviously."

Why wouldn't he have been nominated? Hewson was one of the original founders of the camps. He planned out where to get food and water, organized the meal prep, and how to handle the animals and crops. He'd been integral to everyone's survival for the past three years.

"Who else?" Drew pressed.

"From this camp, me and Danny." Hewson watched as Beck and Drew exchanged glances.

Drew shook his head. "Danny is a good guy, but you and I both know Beck would've been voted in over him."

That was exactly what Hewson didn't want to happen. In fact, that was one of the main reasons he didn't wait for them to return before the vote.

Beck's eyes were still narrowed in on him. "It's awfully convenient you elected leaders while I was gone."

"Face it, Beck, you lost. You don't have a say in how we move forward, and it pisses you off. Frankly, I'm thrilled I don't have to deal with you. It couldn't have worked out better for me."

Beck stepped toward him, trying to use his height as intimidation, but Hewson wouldn't back down. Beck was harmless—basically a boy in a man's body. Sure, people liked him, but he didn't have what it took to be a leader. He needed more backbone, an attitude of *I'll do whatever it takes to get the job done.* Hewson was the one with those qualities. That was why people had looked to him for leadership for the past three years.

"I wouldn't count me out just yet," Beck said. "I'm never out of anything."

He wasn't only referring to the rebuild. He was talking about Novah, too.

Hewson's body tensed. "Stay away from my sister."

"I didn't say anything about your sister."

"We both know what you meant. If you know what's good for you, you'll leave her alone."

"Is that a threat?"

"It's not a request."

They exchanged heated glares, the tension growing as each second passed.

"As I said"—Beck took a few steps back—"I wouldn't count me out." Then, he turned and walked away.

Hewson had to hold himself back from running after him and tackling Beck to the ground. But things had changed. Hewson was on the rebuild committee. If he played his cards right, he could set himself up to be the leader of whatever new nation they formed. He just had to keep his eyes on the prize and not let Beck Haslett bring him down.

"I can't stand that guy," he muttered. The tightness in his shoulders dissipated, and his clenched fingers relaxed.

Drew shook his head before walking away, too. "You don't like anyone."

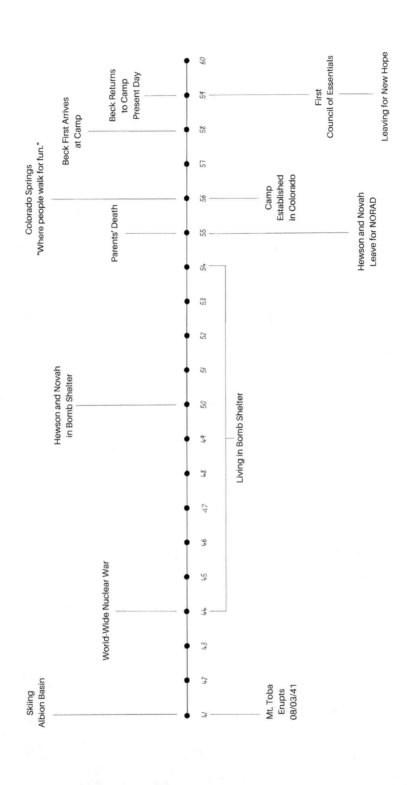

Skiing
Albion Basin

Colorado Springs
"Where people walk for fun."

Beck First Arrives
at Camp

Beck Returns
to Camp
Present Day

World-Wide Nuclear War

Hewson and Novah
in Bomb Shelter

Parents' Death

Camp
Established
in Colorado

First
Council of Essentials

Hewson and Novah
Leave for NORAD

Leaving for New Hope

Living in Bomb Shelter

Mt. Toba
Erupts
08/03/41

41 42 43 44 45 46 47 48 49 50 51 52 53 54 55 56 57 58 59 60

6

Beck

Summer 2059 - Present Day

Danny poked the fire with a long stick. Six yellow squash hung above the flames. It wasn't even close to enough food for the people in this camp for lunch, but portions had been rationed. Beck didn't plan on taking a bite. Skipping meals was nothing new. It was more important that other people got a meal. He would eat...*eventually*.

"I want to be a part of the rebuild plans." Beck looked squarely at Danny. "How can I get in on it?"

Danny gave him a sideways glance under his cowboy hat. "I ain't going to give you my spot."

"I'm not asking for it. I think you need to be involved." Danny had a lot of experience in life. His knowledge was invaluable. "I just want to be involved, too."

Danny straightened, giving his back a rest from leaning over the fire. "We need you, kid. You've got good ideas, and people like your optimism. But at this point, I don't see how we could revote."

Beck played with the stubble on his chin. "What if I was added in as the seventh person? I wouldn't be taking anyone's spot."

"That wouldn't be fair. Who's to say that anyone else couldn't just add themselves after you? Where would it stop?"

Danny was right. There had to be some order to the process.

"Maybe I could go to each camp and plead my case. Explain that I wasn't here when the vote happened and didn't get a fair chance to be included."

"That could work, but you'd need a heck of a lot of people to agree that you should be included if you're going to have any chance of convincing Hewson. Y'all are like oil and water."

He would need the majority of all three camps combined so that Hewson couldn't refute it.

"Even then, it ain't going to be easy. You'll have to convince the other six elected leaders that were voted in, but you'll never get Hewson on board."

Beck glanced at Hewson across the camp. He stood over a raging bonfire, melting scraps of metal.

"And if I were you"—Danny pointed his stick at Beck —"I'd stay away from Novah. That girl will get your butt in trouble. Hewson will never warm up to you if you're wooing his little sister."

"Wooing, huh?" Beck grinned. "That sounds exciting."

Danny laughed. "You're a twitter-pated idiot, but I can't say I blame you. I felt the same way when I first met Emily. That woman had me wrapped around her finger for fifty years." Danny smiled as if he was lost in the past. "Man, I'd give anything to have her here with me."

"What happened to her?"

"Smoke inhalation from a wildfire. I guess that's better than the actual flames burning her alive." His eyes dropped to the fire in front of him. "I just thought I would be able to protect her, and I hate that I couldn't."

"Desolation is bigger than all of us." Beck offered a comforting smile. "Sometimes we have to accept that."

It had taken Beck years to accept that reality himself.

After his mother and sisters were taken in the flood, something inside him snapped. He refused to believe that they were dead. He just needed to find them, and he wouldn't rest until he did. But instead of finding his family, he found other survivors that he could help and protect. Eventually, he had to face the fact that no matter how hard he worked, he wasn't going to bring his mom and sisters back. Desolation took them, and there was nothing he could do about it. He had to move on and help where he could.

"Life is just not the same without Emily." Danny glanced at Beck. "So maybe I understand a little bit why you can't just walk away from Novah." He pointed his stick at him again. "But I still think you're an idiot."

"Who's an idiot?" Drew asked, coming into the conversation. He took a seat on the stump next to Beck.

"Beck," Danny snapped. "He's still all hung up on Novah. You'd think the boy would've learned his lesson last year."

Beck laughed. "Don't worry. I've learned my lesson."

That was mostly true.

He still planned to try again with Novah, but this time, he'd sneak around better.

See? He'd learned a lot.

"Have you ever heard of Romeo and Juliet?" Drew asked, stretching his feet toward the fire.

"Of course." A flash of a memory whipped through Beck's mind. He was just a boy. His mother's gentle face huddled next to his as they bent over the pages of a tattered book. Beck could still see the book's title, feel the embossed letters on his fingertips, *The Works of William Shakespeare*.

"This is my favorite story," his mother had exclaimed, her excitement contagious as she turned the pages of *Romeo and Juliet*. It was one of the few memories Beck still had of his mother.

"What does that have to do with anything?" Beck questioned.

Drew smiled. "Well, Novah and Hewson are the Capulets, and you, my friend, are part of the Montague family—Hewson's bitter enemy."

"That's ridiculous. Hewson's not my bitter enemy." He sucked in the truth with his next breath. "I just don't like how he treats Novah."

"Either way, Romeo, you need to keep away from Juliet," Drew joked.

"Trust us on this one," Danny added. "Nothing good can come of it."

Something good *could* come of it if Novah loved him, too.

That was why Beck couldn't give up.

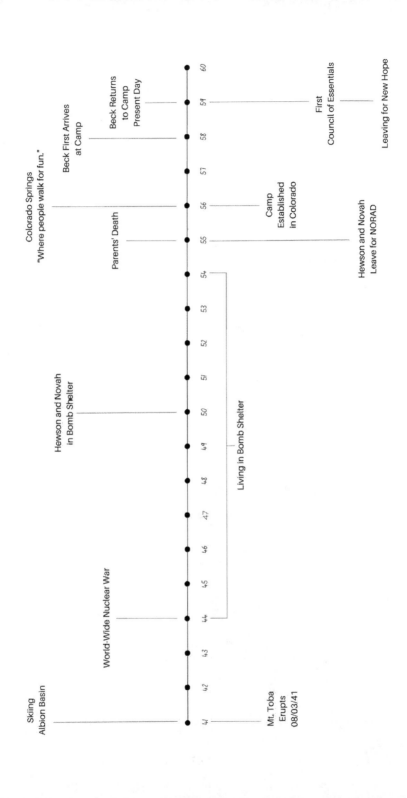

7

Novah

Fall 2055 - Four Years Ago

"Novah, you heard the radio," Hewson argued. "They want all survivors listening to make their way to NORAD in Colorado Springs."

"We heard that message in the bomb shelter almost two years ago. You don't even know if that's still the plan."

"That's why we continue to listen, in case there's a new message."

Ever since their dad had taught Hewson how to use that stupid hand-cranked emergency radio, he'd been obsessed with it. If Novah had to listen to one more second of static, she might stick a sharp object in her ear to permanently damage her eardrums just to put her out of her misery.

"I don't even know what NORAD means," Novah

spat, glaring at her brother. They'd finally returned to Kansas after ten years of living in the bomb shelter. Granted, it didn't look anything like the place she'd remembered from her childhood. Between the tornados, floods, and fires, nothing was the same, but she wanted to stay there even if it killed her.

"NORAD: North American Aerospace Defense Command." Novah felt like she was in some sort of history lesson. "It's a government bunker buried deep in the mountains of Colorado. We'll be safe from natural disasters there. The government is calling for survivors. We need to go."

"How are we even going to get there?" She was sick of everything being so difficult, and traveling hundreds of miles to Colorado sounded difficult.

"We're going to walk."

Obviously.

There was no other way to get there or anywhere.

Her eyes narrowed in anger. "I can't walk. Remember?"

Hewson shook his head in exasperation. "And whose fault is that?"

He was right.

He was *always* right.

It had only been eight months since they'd lost their parents, and it was all Novah's fault. Plus, she'd managed to hurt her foot in the process. She was a liability, a hindrance to survival.

"Novah, I've given you eight months to recover. It's time to get going again. We can't stay here forever."

"I don't want to go. Just leave me behind." She swiped at a tear that had found a way out.

Hewson threw his hands up. "I'm not leaving you behind! You're coming to NORAD with me whether you like it or not."

Novah's eyes went sharp, a weak attempt to stand her ground. After everything that had happened, she should've been grateful Hewson was still willing to drag her along with him. She needed to stop making everything so difficult for him.

"We're going to live inside that bunker, and we're going to survive this hell." He pushed his hair back. "We'll survive and wait until all the natural disasters stop, because it has to stop. Nature can't keep hitting us like this."

The fire in Hewson's eyes was the same fire that had gotten them this far. It would also get them to NORAD, no matter how much she didn't want to go. She could continue to argue with him, but the outcome would be the same.

She had no choice.

She owed Hewson this.

She owed Hewson *everything*.

She was headed to Colorado.

But what was the point of going to NORAD? Novah didn't even want to survive. Maybe if she was lucky, she'd be swept into a tornado of her own.

Novah

Summer 2059 - Present Day

One hundred sixty-eight newcomers arrived yesterday with Drew and Beck's search party. Excitement always came with the addition of new survivors, but this time felt different. People seemed happier, livelier, and it all centered around Beck's return.

He was just that kind of guy—the one you could count on for a positive word of encouragement when it seemed like all hope was lost, a funny joke, or an entertaining story. Novah didn't know how he did it. Optimism and happiness oozed out of him with every breath while the rest took it one breath at a time. Everything about the situation at camp was awful. They were literally living during the worst time in history—worse than Noah's Ark time. Heavy rain that flooded everything would've been a welcomed way to die. But knowing Beck, he would've built an ark right alongside Noah and saved the day for hundreds of people then like he did now. She'd lost count of how many people he'd rescued from the wreckage of Desolation and brought to camp.

Novah pushed a needle and string through Hewson's shirt, fixing a small hole. She repeated the up-and-down process one more time before glancing up, her gaze finding Beck. He sat close to the fire, talking with Danny and Drew. Her thoughts had circled back to him every few seconds since he'd arrived—including all night long.

It was stupid.

Thinking about Beck was like playing with matches. Someone was bound to get burned. Actually, they were *both* going to get burned if she didn't get her treacherous thoughts under control. She tried to ignore him, not glance in his direction to see what he was doing or who he was talking to. She was doing good. She hadn't looked his way for at least ten seconds—a personal record. But after those long ten seconds, her eyes gravitated, as always, back to him.

This has to stop!

She stood, deciding right then and there that this was a good day to do laundry in the river. Not that they had that many clothes to wash. She and Hewson each had a change of clothes, and that was it, but the chore was an excuse to get in the cool mountain water and an excuse to get away from Beck. The sun was shining. The air was hot. It was the perfect plan.

Novah grabbed their clothes and headed up the trail to the water. A couple of years ago, Hewson had marked a pathway to a spot along the river where the water was calmer. This became where people bathed and did laundry without the fear of getting swept away in the current. There was also another path that led farther up the river. That was where their camp gathered water for drinking and cooking.

Novah sat on the bank, rolling her jeans up past her

calves. She nodded to an older woman who gathered her things to leave. It looked like Novah would have the stream to herself for a few moments, which was exactly how she liked it.

Where Hewson thrived on being the leader, Novah just wanted to stand in the back and not have to talk to anyone. It wasn't that she was shy or had social anxiety. She just didn't have anything to say. She was a listener, always content to be in the crowd, not in front of it. Every big personality needed someone like her. That was probably why she and Hewson worked so well together. He took center stage while she was behind the curtain.

Novah hobbled over the smooth rocks submerged just below the clear water, slowly making her way to her favorite boulder in the center of the river. The rock was flat on top and was the perfect table for her pile of laundry. She leaned against the side of the boulder, taking the pressure off her bad ankle. Then, she grabbed Hewson's ratty green t-shirt. She smiled to herself, examining the hole in the armpit that she'd now fixed.

The cold liquid tickled over her bare legs. Tall pine trees surrounded her, smelling fresh, reminding her it was summer. It was a miracle these trees had even survived the years of atypical weather and natural disasters. She respected their resilience. She wished she had a little more of that in herself.

Despite the fact that she'd grown accustomed to living on the benches of the Cheyenne Mountains, she wouldn't say she was happy—mostly just going through the motions. But she couldn't deny that being here at camp was better than anywhere else they'd been the last few years. When Hewson told her, four years ago, that they had to make their way to Colorado, she thought he was crazy. But it was Hewson. He was her older brother, so she'd gone along with it. And in the end, he'd been right. This was what was best for them.

Something pink and red smacked against Novah's face and then dropped perfectly into her hands as if she meant to catch whatever it was. Her eyes tried to make sense of it as they studied the fabric.

"You're welcome."

She looked up. Beck stepped into the water with a satisfied smile. His shirt was off, and he had stripped down to navy-blue boxers. The rest of his clothes were left back on the bank. She scanned the area for Hewson like she always did, even though she knew he wouldn't be there.

They were alone for the first time in a year, causing the steady beat of her heart to pulse in her ears. Maybe it was because the last time they were alone together— besides when she broke up with him—Beck had kissed her. It was a mind-blowing, knock-your-socks-off, make-you-go-weak-in-the-knees kind of kiss. Now, here he was —*shirtless*—an equally mind-blowing, knock-your-socks-off, make-you-go-weak-in-the-knees kind of experience.

Everyone needed to bathe. Sometimes they had to do it in front of others. It was typical for Novah to see men undressed. It was the nature of survival at camp. What wasn't typical was how she felt when she saw Beck with his shirt off. He looked just as good as she'd remembered —and boy, had she remembered.

He was lean—*everyone* was—but his body still had defined muscles that struck the perfect balance between strength and sexiness. His arms and legs were strong and defined, and his skin was evenly bronzed, like he'd spent every day that summer with his shirt off. That was the only plausible explanation for the absence of a harsh farmer's tan.

The buzzing in Novah's stomach started up again as she watched Beck walk toward her with his dazzling smile. Charity, an older girl from when they lived in the bomb shelter, once referred to good-looking men as *eye candy*. At the time, her description made no sense, but now Novah understood the meaning all too well.

Beck's playful smile tilted higher as if he could read her *eye candy* thoughts.

She glanced down at the fabric in her hands, trying to remember what he'd just said to her. "What?"

"You're welcome," Beck said the words slower this time, as if that would help with her confusion.

Her head popped up, meeting his gaze. "For what?"

"Your new underwear." He pointed to the pink-and-red thing in her hands.

She lifted the item with both hands to see what it was. It had been years since she'd seen underwear like this. The fabric was pink with red-trimmed edges. On the front, written in red cursive, was the word *sexy*. Novah peeked around the panties to see Beck holding back a laugh.

"Do you like them?" he asked with raised eyebrows.

She didn't know what to say. She hadn't had new underwear in quite a while. Her current ones had multiple holes, and where there wasn't a hole, there were stains from her monthly cycle. So, yes, she liked them, but she didn't want Beck to know that.

She eyed him. "I could do without the sexy part."

"Well, considering the type of store I was in, that's pretty mild."

"I see." She bit her lip, determined not to let a smile break loose.

Beck lifted his hand, rubbing the thick stubble that coated his chin. He stood there like he had nothing better to do than to watch her.

Novah dropped her eyes. She had no desire to engage in a staring contest with him. She glanced at the laundry she still hadn't washed. All she wanted now was to get back to camp and back to more regular heartbeats.

"Is there something else I can help you with?" Maybe that would prompt him to leave.

He shrugged. "I was just waiting for you to say thank you—you know, for your new underwear."

"I've never thanked a man for underwear before. That seems creepy." She smirked despite her best efforts.

Beck let out a big laugh, and Novah couldn't hold her smile in any longer.

"Too much underwear talk is creepy, but"—a

mischievous grin spread across his lips—"in the future, *some* underwear talk might be considered foreplay."

"I hate to disappoint you, Beck"—she leaned forward, dropping her voice to a playful whisper—"but we're never talking about underwear again." She straightened and repeated, *"Never."* If Hewson could hear her now, he'd probably try to ground her as if she were a teenager.

"I refuse to believe that," Beck said with a cocky smile. Did charisma and confidence have to accompany everything he said? It just made him all the more irresistible.

A piece of the wall Novah had built around her heart crumbled to the ground. She couldn't afford to lose any more. She had to keep her feelings fenced in. It was the only way to protect herself.

"I followed you here, you know." He lifted his shoulders like what he'd just admitted was a little embarrassing. "I've been waiting for a chance to talk to you ever since I got back."

"Well, I'm almost done, so it doesn't look like it's going to work out." Novah picked up a shirt and plunged it into the water. Looking busy was the first step to avoidance.

"Then I guess I'll have to settle for just washing my hair." He took the tie out from around his bun, letting his hair fall almost to his shoulders. "Landon, the botanist from California, taught me how to use soap plants to bathe with." He held up a brown bulb between his fingers. "This is my first time trying it."

Novah's eyes shot to the plant. How did Beck have so many friends in different camps? She knew of the older man, Landon. Everyone did. Landon was in charge of planting and growing all the crops, but Novah had never talked to him before. He lived in camp three and was intimidating.

"I'll share some soap with you." Beck's lips curled into a devilish smile. "You wash my back. I'll wash yours."

She raised her eyebrows as a warning.

"What?" He flashed an innocent smile like he was harmless, but nothing about what Beck suggested seemed harmless.

Novah pushed the image of lathering up his back and torso out of her head and laid out the green t-shirt on the rock. Next, she picked up Hewson's pants.

"Thanks for the offer, but I have to get the laundry done." She didn't *have to* get the laundry done, but what else was she going to say? It was too dangerous to strike up a conversation with him.

"Can I bring my clothes over for you to wash, too?"

"Everyone washes their own clothes." She kept her focus on scrubbing.

"Except Hewson." He pointed to the pants she'd just dunked underwater.

His remark irritated her. Why did everything have to be about their stupid rivalry?

"Hewson does a lot around camp for *everybody*. The least I could do is wash his clothes for him."

"I was only joking, Novah."

"I know." She used the side of a flat rock to scrub a stain.

Beck splashed some water over his body and hair, momentarily pausing their conversation. "How have you been this last year?"

She paused washing, watching as water dripped from his hair and rolled down his chest and biceps. She shook her head, refusing to let the sight stay in her mind.

"We don't need to do this."

He extended his arm, scrubbing his skin with his other hand. "Do what?"

"Talk."

"Why can't we talk?" His smile was so charming she felt the need to crouch down again and scrub. Anything to avoid focusing on his handsome lips. "Aren't we friends?"

Novah shook her head.

"We're not friends?" Amusement filled his voice.

"No."

"What about friends with benefits?"

She gave him a sideways glance just in time to see the corner of his mouth raise. "Definitely not that."

"Enemies?"

She smirked, dropping her focus to the pants once again. "No."

He walked toward where she was and crouched down

beside her. Her breath stilled with his closeness. His head dipped, putting him in her eyesight. "Then, what are we?"

She looked at Beck—his patient eyes, wet hair, glistening muscles, kind smile—and wanted nothing more than to lean forward and bury her head in his neck. He'd rub her back and reassure her that he was there and that everything would be okay. He'd hold her and make her *feel* again, and that was the biggest thing that scared her. *Feeling* meant getting hurt.

"Nothing." She lifted her chin. "We're nothing."

His gaze was firm yet fragile, and the last thing Novah wanted was to break Beck's heart again. But then, something playful stirred in his eyes.

"Fine, then." He masked his hurt with a smile. "We won't talk."

He stood but didn't back away. Instead, he bathed right next to her, running his fingers through his hair and scrubbing his scalp. His raised arms accentuated the muscles on the side of his chest and back. Talking would have been better than *this*.

Novah decided right then that their clothes were clean enough.

She gathered up her things, including the new underwear—she was for sure going to keep them—and started to wade through the water, trying to escape Beck and his soapy muscles. But nothing was ever that easy. Her bad foot got tripped up on an unstable rock, and she lost her balance, falling into Beck's arms, who somehow was there to save the day. Novah's hands gripped his wet body, using him for support as she straightened to a stand. His fingers clung to her waist to keep things steady.

Everything was stable now.

The situation was under control.

The threat of falling was gone.

But neither of them moved, as if they both craved the closeness.

Novah's gaze stayed low, watching the rise and fall of his chest and the chills covering his skin. His thumbs slipped under her shirt, slowly drawing circles on the edges of her hipbones. If she stood still, maybe she could keep her heartbeat from running wild. Maybe she could ignore the heat flaming hcr skin.

"I've missed you." His words came out like an agonizing plea.

Cautiously, her eyes shifted to his face. Beck's head was dipped down, leaving only inches between their two lips, but instead of kissing her, he gently pressed his forehead against hers. Novah's eyes shut as his protective arms closed in around her.

"I..." he began to say, letting out a nervous laugh. "I'm a little out of practice flirting with you." Through her half-hooded eyes, she saw the boyish smile that formed over his lips. "Next time, I promise I'll do better."

The words *next time* and *flirting* made her stomach cartwheel, adding to the intense feelings of his touch. It all felt so...*amazing*.

Novah couldn't do this. She couldn't fall for Beck all over again just to lose him. Her heart needed to remain in lockdown mode. That was the only way to stay strong.

She pulled back, releasing herself from him. "I've got to go."

"Please don't." He reached his arm out to her, but she turned and kept moving until her feet reached the moist dirt of the bank.

She made a split-second decision that she'd inevitably regret later.

She glanced over her shoulder at Beck.

He looked sincere and safe, with a hopeful smile that seeped into the corners of her heart.

How did that happen?

Novah had so carefully built a wall around it.

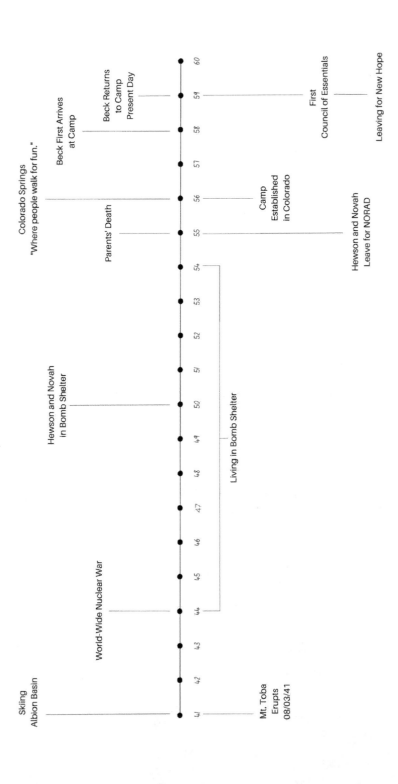

8

Beck

Summer 2059 - Present Day

They had a meager dinner of potatoes—the one crop that was thriving in bulk. Beck savored the sweet taste of food in his mouth as he listened to groups of people chatting around him.

"Are you finished?" Aycee asked, nodding at the bowl in his hands.

Aycee Trainor was in her late twenties. Tall and slim, with auburn hair. She had a cute smile that curved higher on one side, leading up to a dimple, like a dot over a lowercase I. They found her with a group of people in Missouri eight months ago.

"I can take that for you." She smiled.

"Thank you." Beck placed his dish in her hands and watched as she walked away.

"What I wouldn't give to be young and handsome

again." Drew chuckled beside him. "To have all the girls begging to clean up after me."

"Ah, you're still young—just not handsome," Beck teased.

"Not young enough for those ladies." Drew nodded to the group of twenty-something women washing out bowls and spoons. "Rumor has it they're all in love with you."

"Not all of them." Beck's eyes darted to Novah. She stood by the other women, washing plates and bowls.

Their conversation by the river earlier that day hadn't gone terrible. The corner of Beck's mouth lifted as he thought back to the moment when she fell into his arms. There was nothing terrible about that. But Novah had been guarded. Just like she was when he'd first met her. Most men would be discouraged by her repeated attempts to push him away. But Beck wasn't a quitter. He'd wear her down...eventually.

Drew followed his stare to Novah. "I warned you about that one."

"I know."

"What about Aycee? She seems sweet on you."

"She's nice." Beck switched his gaze to her.

Aycee was nice and happy and easy, but for some reason, he wasn't interested. He didn't feel that spark with her or any other woman besides Novah. She was the only woman he'd ever had feelings for as a grown man. People love who they love. It's an unexplainable human emotion that nobody can turn off or on whenever they feel like it.

"Who is everybody's celebrity crush?" Aycee asked the group.

"Celebrity crushes are stupid," Hewson barked from across the fire. "All those people are dead now."

"It's still fun even if they're dead," Aycee defended. "Besides, you don't have to answer if you don't want to."

"You're right." Hewson stood. "I don't want to answer." He stomped away, showing the group his disapproval of the topic choice, but no one seemed to care that he left. He was such a jerk. At least he was consistent.

Danny surprised everyone by chiming in. "Y'all are probably too young to know this one, but I sure loved Zendaya when I was a teenager."

"Oh, I've heard of her!" Aycee beamed as she dried dishes. "My mom had a few old Blu-rays of some of her shows. *The Greatest...*"

"*Showman*," Danny finished. "She was somethin'."

"What about you, Beck?" Aycee asked. "What celebrity do you have a crush on?"

Drew eyed him with a teasing smile, as if he thought this entire conversation was a way for Aycee to talk to him more.

Beck shook off Aycee's question with a polite smile. "I don't really have one."

"Yes, he does." Indie sat up from her spot on the couch across from them. She'd traveled with Beck for ten months. They found her living in a crushed Ford truck in what was left of Tennessee, surviving off of canned food she'd gathered in the wreckage. Beck respected her. She was young—almost eighteen—but she was resourceful, surviving out there on her own.

Beck looked at her, confused. "I do?"

"Yes!" Her eyes brimmed with mischievousness. "Beck has a crush on Zan Hughes!"

"But that's a boy," Aycee said. "Last time I checked, Beck was straight."

"I know, but he carries around a crumpled-up magazine cutout of Zan Hughes." Indie giggled. "There are hearts all over it and everything. I saw a glimpse of it before he got embarrassed and pulled it away."

Everyone around them laughed, but Beck's eyes pulled to Novah. She didn't look back at him, but her movements had stilled, and even in the dim light of the setting sun, Beck thought he saw a blush creep up her cheeks.

If he was being honest, he had a slight hue of pink covering his face, too. He'd never planned on Novah knowing that he'd taken her paper out of the fire and carried it with him all this time.

"Explain yourself," someone teased.

Beck shrugged, not even bothering to summon up something funny to say. "That picture's special. It reminds me of someone I care for."

Novah finally peeked over at him. She didn't seem mad or upset. It was hard to tell, but it seemed like she was a little flattered.

"That's so sweet that you carry something special with you." Aycee's words broke the moment, and Novah glanced down once again.

"I heard you used that fancy soap plant today." Indie moved from her spot on the couch and plopped down on the log next to Beck and Drew. "I want to smell your hair and see if that soap plant really works." She leaned over, brushing the tip of her nose into Beck's bun. "That's the best you've ever smelled," she teased, like a little sister—like his little sisters would've if they were still alive.

She hopped excitedly to her feet. Beck wasn't sure what Indie was up to, but the mischievous glint in her eyes said she was scheming.

She turned over her shoulder. "Novah, you've got to come and smell Beck's hair."

Oh, so this was what Indie was up to. Beck glanced at Drew again, who obviously had caught the drift, too. How could he not? She was matchmaking harder than those stupid dating apps his parents had used years ago. Beck never should've told Indie about Novah and his feelings for her. But when they were out in the desolate terrain, it seemed like they would never make it back to camp. Her knowing about his crush—okay, more than a crush—seemed harmless at the time. But Indie must've noticed how they'd just looked at each other and put together that the Zan Hughes paper was really Novah's.

Now, Beck was full of regrets.

"I don't want to smell Beck's hair," Novah said. "I'm

busy." Much to his disappointment, her eyes never left the dish she held.

Indie grabbed Beck's hand and pulled him up, dragging him toward Novah. He had to give it to the young girl; she was determined. This was her not-so-subtle way of forcing Novah to talk to him.

"Seriously, Novah. He smells *so* good." Indie tugged Beck over to her side, depositing him there.

Novah gave him a sideways glance, her face expressionless.

"She doesn't want to smell his hair," Aycee chimed in. "Novah said yesterday that she hates men with long hair. She likes a clean-cut look."

Beck folded his arms across his chest, staring down at Novah with an amused smile. "Really?" But she pursed her lips together, refusing to comment.

"Yeah, she cuts Hewson's hair all the time. She said she doesn't want him to look like a lumberjack." Aycee looked at Novah to confirm. "Right?"

"What do you have against lumberjacks?" Beck shifted his weight, fully entertained by this new discovery.

Novah momentarily turned to him. "Everything."

"That's not how I remember it." He pushed up one playful brow. "I seem to remember you liking lumberjack-type men. You know, men who are good with an ax."

"Not ones with hair like yours."

Beck couldn't hold in his laughter. She was fighting her own smile as well.

"What's wrong with my hair?"

Her focus went to the dishes as she bit back her smile. "I don't like it."

"Well, we can't have that."

Seriously.

He couldn't have that.

It was already an uphill battle with Novah. He needed his looks to at least help his chances. Not hurt them. He couldn't just rely on his charming personality. It wasn't enough. This was an all-hands-on-deck situation.

Beck stepped back, addressing the people around them. "Does anybody have scissors?"

"Each camp has some. I'll get ours." A rough-looking woman with several missing teeth scurried away.

"You're not really thinking about cutting off your hair, are you?" Aycee gasped.

"I sure am. I haven't had a haircut in over a year. Which is really a shame because I'm kind of fond of haircuts...as long as I have a stylist I like and she's not too distracted to do a good job." He flashed Novah a playful smile, trying to remind her of the last time she'd cut his hair a year and a half ago. She'd definitely been distracted back then with all the kissing they'd done in between cuts. Beck was surprised he'd walked away looking semi-decent. Back then, there wasn't a wedge between them or their relationship. Their feelings were new and uncomplicated.

He'd give anything to go back to that time. Maybe

this haircut would help Novah feel the same way—remind her of better times.

The mangy woman returned, placing scissors in Beck's hand.

"What do you say?" He raised his eyebrows.

She tilted her head, considering it.

"Please, cut my hair so I don't look like a lumberjack anymore." Beck had no problem begging.

"Come on, Novah," Indie encouraged. "I can't picture Beck without a bun. It will be fun."

She hesitated. Her eyes glanced around. To anyone else it would seem like she was just looking at the gathering crowd, but Beck knew she was really watching for Hewson. When she decided the coast was clear, she grabbed the scissors, eliciting a clap from Indie.

"I make no promises that you'll look better."

"But we both know that I probably will." Beck grinned, watching her tie her brown hair back into a knot.

Someone brought over a stump for him to sit on, and he started unbuttoning his shirt.

"What are you doing?" Novah panicked.

"I don't want to get hair all over my shirt."

"No." She folded her arms, shaking her head. "Uh-uh."

"Oh, come on, Novah," Aycee complained. She raised her fist in the air, chanting, "Take it off! Take it off!"

More women joined in. "Take it off! Take it off!"

His eyes danced, and he lowered his voice so only she could hear. "I was shirtless last time you cut my hair. You didn't seem to have a problem with it then."

Novah glared at him. "I'd be careful if I were you. I'm the one holding a sharp object."

"Alright. Alright." Beck raised his hands, quieting the group of women. "The shirt stays on per the request of my hair stylist."

A few women groaned around him.

"It's fine." He took a seat on the stump.

Novah walked behind him, pulling at strands. "How short do you want it?"

He closed his eyes, savoring the feeling of her fingers in his hair. "Let's go for the clean-cut look you like so much. Or whatever you think. I just want *you* to like it."

She puffed out an irritated laugh and dramatically chopped off a piece. The girls around him gasped as the long strand fell to the ground.

"You just jumped right in, didn't you?"

"Isn't that what you wanted?" She pulled at another strand, clipping it away from his head.

"Should I be worried you're going to make me look worse than I do now?"

"Probably," she said impassively, which made Beck smile.

Novah continued to cut, running her fingers through his hair repeatedly. He reveled in the feeling, enjoying every second like it was the last time she would ever touch him. Obviously, he hoped it wasn't, but he never knew with Novah.

Without Beck in the conversation, the group of chatty girls lost interest and scattered, leaving them alone. He tried to keep his breathing even, not let his attraction for her run wild, but then she moved in front of him. He dropped his eyes—it was the gentlemanly thing to do. But his restraint was tested when her legs split his. They were thigh to thigh, and all Beck wanted to do was grab her by the waist and pull her down to him so he could look into her eyes, hug her to him, and kiss her lips. They'd spent a year apart from each other, and now his want for her was at an all-time high. But for now, he'd have to settle for just dreaming about touching her.

"What are you smiling about?" She raised an incriminating brow.

Was he smiling? She'd caught him in the middle of his reverie.

"I was just thinking."

"About what?"

"You." He glanced up, meeting her gaze. "*Holding you.*"

Her fingers paused as they stared at each other.

"You're wasting your time." Her attention went back to cutting. "I'm not interested."

"Really?" He scooted his legs apart more so his knee brushed up against the side of her leg. Her hands faltered, but she didn't move away.

"Really."

"I'm going to have to try harder, then."

"Is that what this is about? The chase?"

"This has nothing to do with the chase." Beck grasped her arm, forcing her to stop and look at him. "And you know it."

Her chest lifted, and her breath caught in the back of her throat. Beck knew her well enough to know those were the small clues that she felt the same way he did.

She opened her mouth to speak. "I—"

"What's going on here?" Hewson snapped.

Novah jumped out of Beck's grasp.

"What does it look like?" Beck replied coolly.

"I'm giving Beck a haircut." She went back to work as if she were the world's biggest busy bee.

Hewson glared at them both, but Novah avoided his gaze. She was busy, busy, busy.

"Do you want one, too?" There was so much fake innocence in her voice that she was condemning herself. "I'm almost done."

Hewson shook his head, keeping his eyes on Beck. "No."

She clipped a few more pieces, ruffled his hair, then abruptly turned away. "All finished."

Beck stood, smiling with cockiness back at Hewson. He'd said he would stay away from him, but the guy was too easy to upset. He raked his fingers through his short hair, turning to Novah.

"You left it longer than I thought you would."

She looked down, brushing off the hair from her

shirt. "I thought you might want it the same way I used to cut it."

"And I thought you liked a man with a clean-cut look."

He was calling her bluff.

"What I like doesn't matter."

"See, I knew deep down you had a thing for lumberjacks."

"Hardly." She handed him the scissors. "I'm not sure the cut helped." She shrugged, but Beck saw the smirk on her face before she turned and walked away.

Man, he liked her.

No, he *loved* her.

He glanced away from her retreating back, noticing how Hewson watched him.

Beck should try to be more discreet with his feelings. But being discreet wasn't one of his strengths.

9

Beck

Spring 2058 - A Year and a Half Ago

Beck lifted his arms, swinging an ax above his head and bringing the blade down hard on the dead tree. Splinters of wood burst into the air and floated to the ground like snowflakes. He bent over and gathered the firewood and threw it onto the sled next to him. A plastic winter sled wasn't the best way to carry kindling down the mountain, but it still had a rope attached to the front, and it was the best Beck could find at camp.

Even though the temperatures were warming, accumulating a stockpile of firewood was an important job. Without it, everyone would freeze to death at night. Beck wanted to be helpful around camp, so he'd spent the last two days hiking along the mountain, looking for fallen trees that he could cut into kindling.

He'd ditched his shirt hours ago. There was no point

in keeping the sweat-soaked fabric on when an endless supply of perspiration trickled down his face, arms, and back. The warm summer sun seemed to mock him while he worked, as if it never planned on letting the earth cool down enough to even warrant a stockpile of firewood.

Beck grabbed the end of the last tree trunk and stood it up, ready to cut it in half. As he raised his ax, movement caught his eyes, and he paused, shifting his gaze.

A smile covered his lips.

It was Novah Harper, of all people.

Beck was too high up the mountain and too far away from camp for this meeting to be a coincidence. She'd sought him out. It was incredible the confidence that little piece of information gave him. After last week's conversation by the river and then on the couch at camp, when she'd stormed away, Beck had decided to give her space. She was the type of person whose trust had to be earned. But there she was, climbing up the mountain with her bad foot just to see him.

"I thought you didn't want to be friends." Beck's playful smile was proof he was teasing.

"I don't." She leaned against a tree to catch her breath. "I just came here to apologize for how I treated you last week."

"You hiked up the mountain on your hurt foot just to apologize?" His brows raised, and so did the corner of his mouth. "It must be a pretty important apology."

"It's not just about the apology. I needed the exercise, too."

She was full of crap, and Beck loved every second of it.

"So, I'm sorry about how rude I was last week. I've just never had anyone interested in being friends, and I guess I don't know how to react. Plus, you ask a lot of personal questions, and I don't know..." She fidgeted with her fingers. "I guess I'm not used to that."

"Apology accepted."

"Just like that?"

Beck lifted his shoulders. "Do you not want me to forgive you?"

"No, I do." She scratched the side of her neck. "I'm glad we got that cleared up. I guess I'll go, then."

"Now wait a minute. You don't need to run off so fast...or *slow*, depending on how much your foot hurts." She smiled, okay with how he joked about her injury. "Come on over here." He waved her to him. "You can cut the last piece of wood."

"Me?" Novah's head kicked back. "I can't cut wood."

He held the ax out to her. "Why not?"

Her eyes dropped to her foot.

"I'm not Hewson," he said. "And I'm not going to tell you what you can or can't do. I think you can manage your limitations all on your own."

A wrestle of emotion played across her face, and just when Beck thought she was about to blame her bad ankle, she pushed off the tree and walked toward him.

"Fine. Show me how."

"Yes, ma'am."

She grabbed the ax from him, a small smirk toying on her lips. "Don't call me ma'am."

"Does my southern charm offend you?"

"No, it makes me feel like I'm eighty years old."

"I could call you *miss*, but it just doesn't have the same ring to it. Especially coming from a lumberjack like myself."

Novah rolled her eyes, but that same smirk on her lips told Beck a lot.

"Now, the first thing you need to know about chopping wood is it's all about the form."

"The form?"

"That's right." He stepped forward, then hesitated. "Do I have permission to approach the student? I mean, you do have an ax in your hand."

Novah smiled. "Permission granted."

Beck stepped behind her, placing his hands on her shoulders. Despite the fact that this was just an innocent wood-chopping lesson, his heart raced with excitement.

"Your feet need to be shoulder-width apart." He gently nudged her body into position. "Then, grip your ax with your dominant hand near the head of the tool." His fingers slowly slid down her arms. He picked up her hands and fitted them over the handle in the correct position. "The most powerful swing happens when you slide your dominant hand down the handle toward your other hand." Their arms moved together, mimicking the movement, gliding up and down the handle. "That's how you deliver a blow powerful enough to cut the wood."

"Am I doing it right?" Novah turned her head, eyeing him over her shoulder. The height difference between them put her face next to his. By this point, Beck's heart was pounding so hard he was sure she could feel it knocking against her shoulder blades. But he didn't care. He didn't even care how sweaty he was or the fact that he probably smelled like BO. All he could think about was how nice it was to have Novah this close to him and feel the flicker of something fun brewing.

"I think you got it. All that's left is to swing it over your head."

Beck didn't want to let go. He'd be more than happy to stand there with his arms around Novah for a few more minutes, but there was no way she could actually chop wood with him hovering over her, so he reluctantly stepped back.

"Let's see what you've got."

There was a hesitation in her eyes, like she didn't really believe she was capable. Novah needed a win like this. She needed to see that, despite her injury, she was just as competent as everyone else. Plus, the fact that the tree was dead and dried out and easier to chop helped her chances.

She sucked in a deep breath and lifted her arms above her head. Her hand drifted down the handle like they practiced as the ax fell toward the log. The blade's tip hit the wood in the center, splitting it in half.

"I did it!" She looked at Beck as if she couldn't believe it had really worked. A bewildered smile drew across her mouth. "I chopped wood. I'm a wood chopper!"

Beck grinned, taking in every moment of her joy.

"What?" She stared back at him.

"This was what I was talking about." He gestured to her. "Your smile just proved my point."

"What?" Her brows lowered in confusion.

"Seeing you smile—for *real*—is more satisfying and rewarding than anything I've ever seen."

That was when Novah laughed, throwing her head back.

"No, wait." Beck laughed, too. "I take it back. Hearing you genuinely laugh is the most rewarding thing."

The cutest pink blush dotted her cheeks. "Stop. Or I'll come after you with this ax."

He held his hands up. "I believe that."

Novah bit her lip, looking around. "So, do you have any more wood for me to chop?"

"That was actually the last one, but…" He pushed his hands into his pockets. "I was going to hike the south mountain tomorrow and gather wood up there. You could always come with me and work on your form."

Work on your form? What is this, a lumberjack competition?

He cleared his throat, trying to find some shred of suaveness. "I mean, you know…if you want to. No pressure or anything like that. Just if you want to get better at chopping wood."

If you want to get better at chopping wood?

There was no suaveness to be found.

He wasn't proud of the jumbled way his words had come out, but asking Novah to spend time with him was like tiptoeing across thin ice. One wrong step and the whole thing would break apart. Novah's willingness to let people in was fragile like that.

"Um…" She chewed the side of her mouth as if it were spearmint gum. "I guess that would be okay," she said, finally looking at him. "The camp needs all the firewood it can get, and that would be a good way for me to help without Hewson breathing down my neck."

Beck didn't care how she spun it in her mind. All he cared about was that Novah had agreed to spend the day with him tomorrow.

It was the beginning of something good.

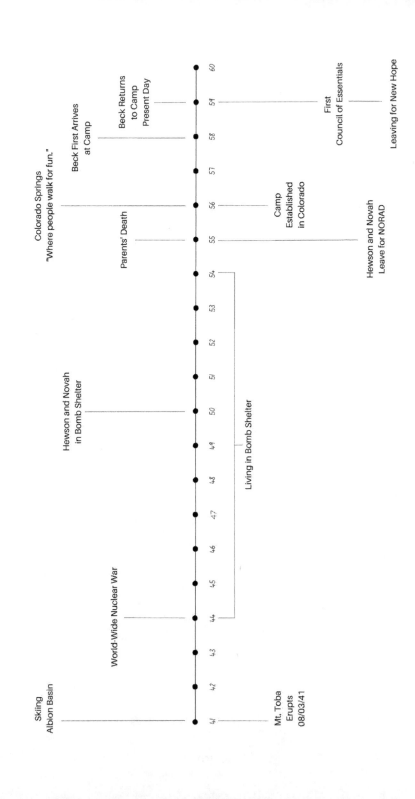

10

Novah

Summer 2059 - Present Day

T*he crying got louder, letting Novah know she was getting closer to the baby. She dug through rubble—a piece of art, the corner of a garage door, a laundry basket, a broken headboard —until she saw the pink baby blanket.*

She bent down, grabbing the baby. "It's okay. You're safe now." She pulled the blanket back to see her face.

The crying stopped, turning into callous laughter. "Made you look!" the baby sneered.

Novah jumped back, dropping the infant. She tried to scoot away, but her ankle was jammed between debris.

Then, her foot snapped in half.

Novah's eyes flew open.

She blinked rapidly, rooting herself to her surroundings.

The cave was dark, but the night sky had already faded into light, with the first signs of dawn shining through the opening.

Her chest collapsed in relief.

Another dream.

She turned her head. Hewson slept peacefully next to her. But there seemed no point in her trying to go back to sleep. Everyone would be waking soon. She slipped on her shoes and slowly made her way out of the cavern.

The morning air cooled her racing heart, causing Novah to shiver as she pulled her shirt around her tighter. She could get breakfast started for everyone, but that wasn't typically her job, so instead, she walked toward the circle of chairs and couches. Her eyes caught the back of Beck's silhouette. He sat on the edge of one of the couches, staring into a cracked hand-held mirror.

Novah shuffled to leave, but it was too late. He'd seen her.

"You're up early," he said in his usual cheerful voice.

"Shh!" She nodded in the direction of the cave and sleeping people behind her.

She shoved her hands into her pockets, walking closer to where he sat. He held his Swiss Army knife up to his cheek, scraping away the last stubble of hair where his beard had been the night before.

"You gave me such a nice haircut last night, I thought

I better shave to match it." His eyes stayed on the mirror in front of him. "What do you think?"

What did she think?

She thought he looked handsome, but she already thought that last night when she'd cut his hair—and every day since she'd met him.

Beck rubbed his hand across his chin, switching the angle so he could examine the other side. His clean face accentuated his strong jaw and cheekbones, giving him a more sophisticated look. Novah was sure no man would like hearing that he had *pretty* lips, but that was what came to mind as she studied him. They were full and curved perfectly over his straight teeth. Without the beard, his already attractive smile would become so much more dangerous.

"It's alright." She acted like she had no desire to run her hands over his smooth skin, even though that was exactly what she wanted to do.

He put the mirror down, finally looking at her. His light-hazel eyes stood out against his now visible face.

"I did it all for you."

"Sorry to have wasted your time." She slunk onto the couch, keeping an entire cushion length between them.

"Nah, I've got nothing but time." He looked across the camp. "Especially if I keep waking up in the middle of the night." He set the mirror and the knife down on the couch and leaned back.

They sat in silence, listening to a rooster from the pasture crow, calling to the sun to rise.

"You said we couldn't talk." He turned to her. "That's why I'm not saying anything to you right now. I just didn't want you to think that I had nothing to say to you...because I do."

She gave him a sideways glance, not even bothering to hold back her small smile. "Thanks for the play-by-play."

"You're welcome."

The silence was thick around them, making Novah's curiosity get the best of her. "If I *did* want to talk, what would you say to me?"

He turned his body toward hers, resting his leg on the cushion between them. "Well, this is only hypothetical, since you don't really want to talk."

"Correct."

"But if we *were* going to talk, I would tell you why I was awake so early. I would tell you I had a dream about my family at the beach. I would remind you that we used to go there every summer until I was ten."

Beck had already told Novah about his family back when they used to spend every day together. She didn't need to hear why they'd stopped vacationing at the beach. The earth's temperature had dropped from all the ash blocking the sun. After the eruption, the beach was too cold for vacations.

"I would also tell you that I'm an expert at making sandcastles."

"And if we *were* talking—which we're not—I would ask

why a dream about going to the beach with your family woke you up." Novah never asked anyone about their families because she didn't want them to ask about hers, but Beck had always eased her anxieties with these kinds of things.

"I would then respond by telling you about my dream, about how my little sisters, Brandi and Bailee, got swept away in the ocean."

Novah knew Beck's story and how his mom and little sisters died in the massive flooding after a tsunami hit North Carolina, but what she didn't know was that he had bad dreams like her. Dreams where his family members died all over again. He'd never mentioned that before.

Novah's voice fell. "I would tell you how sorry I was about your family."

"I know," he whispered, then he continued his carefree banter. "Now, if this were a real conversation— which it's not—I would also tell you that I am excellent at the game horseshoes. Unbeatable."

"Sandcastles and horseshoes?" She raised a teasing eyebrow.

"Yes, I'm quite a man."

"I can see that." She smirked, looking over his handsome face. "I would tell you that I've never played horseshoes before."

"Then I would tell you that you're really missing out." He reached his arm across the back of the couch casually. "The next thing I would do—if we were having a normal conversation—is ask you to tell me something about you that nobody knows."

Novah loved it when Beck played this game. She had to search her mind for something about herself that she hadn't already told him.

He dropped his voice lower, as if he was giving her side instructions. "That's what people do in conversations: say a little bit about themselves, then ask the other person something about them."

"Yes, I know. I've been in conversations before." She smiled at the ridiculousness of it all. "I would tell you that I'm excellent at skiing. At least, the seven-year-old version of me was excellent at skiing."

"I would think that was interesting and ask how a Kansas girl became so good at skiing."

"I would explain that, when I was little, we spent our winter vacations skiing mostly in Colorado but a few times in Utah. That I started skiing as soon as I started walking."

Novah smiled, thinking back to her mother skiing backward, holding her hands, leading her down the bunny hill, and for a moment, she got lost in the memory.

"I hated ski school and refused to go, so my parents took turns teaching me how. I flapped my arms a lot at first and heavily relied on the *pizza* and *French fry* positions, but eventually, I got so good my parents were chasing me down the slopes." She looked at Beck and remembered the game they were playing. Her voice lowered. "That's what I would tell you *if* we were talking."

His eyes were kind like he understood she had difficulty visiting the past. "That would have been a good story to talk about."

They stared at each other, their emotions real even if they pretended the dialogue wasn't. Then, his eyes flickered behind her. Novah turned to see what he was looking at.

Hewson.

He always seemed to find them.

"Thanks for not talking to me." Beck stood. "I know I wouldn't have enjoyed our conversation at all."

She watched him leave, wishing he could've stayed longer.

Hewson collapsed down next to her on the couch. "Why are you always talking to him?"

"We weren't even talking."

"It's like every time I turn around, you're with that guy."

"Two times. I've seen him two times since he's been back." It was actually three, but Hewson didn't need to know about the river yesterday.

"That seems like a lot for three days."

"Beck was the only one out here. What did you want me to do, ignore him?"

"Yes." Hewson pushed a hand through his matted sleep hair.

Novah knew this topic inside and out. Beck was off-limits. It was the official decree cemented into her heart.

"I'm not rude like you." She playfully elbowed him in the ribs, hoping to lighten the mood, maybe even change the subject.

"I hate that guy."

Her elbow jab hadn't accomplished anything she'd wanted it to.

"It's been a year since you've seen him. How can you already hate him again?"

"Easy. He wormed his way into everybody's good graces, and every time I turn around, he's talking to you. It's a repeat of last year. He's trying to turn you against me."

She rolled her eyes. "Not everything is about you, Hewson."

"Trust me. Men like Beck are manipulators. He'll use you and then break your heart."

Novah was the one who had used Beck and broken his heart.

"And just how do you know anything about '*men like Beck*'? Ever since you were fourteen, you've lived in a bomb shelter."

"Just don't disobey me again, okay?"

"Disobey?" Novah raised her eyebrows. "I'm not a little girl anymore."

"I mean it, Novah. Anyone but him."

She looked at her brother and saw the intense way

Hewson stared at her. She'd seen that expression from him most of her life.

As tempting as Beck was, she'd already chosen Hewson. It was her payment for what had happened to their parents. If she gave her brother this, maybe she'd stop feeling like she owed him for the rest of her life.

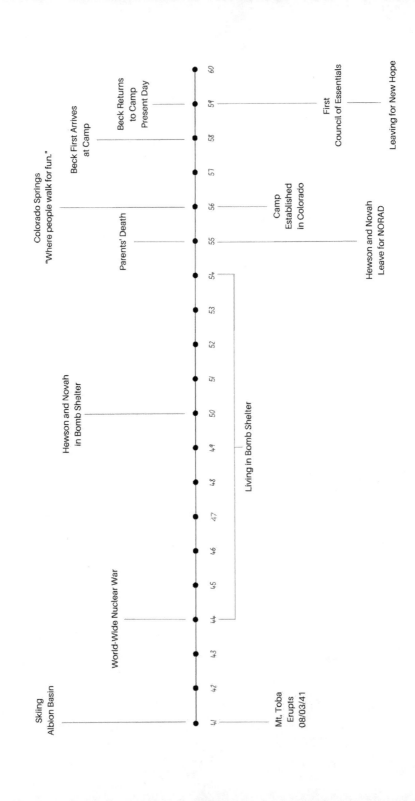

11

Novah

Spring 2058 - A Year and a Half Ago

"Where do you think you're sneaking off to?" Hewson stepped out of the cave just as Novah finished tying her shoes.

The west half of the sky was tinted with orange and pink as the sun crept up. But the camps wouldn't see the light or feel the heat until much later—the mountains hid them in their shadows.

Novah straightened, looking at her brother. "I'm not sneaking off."

False.

She'd purposely gotten up early so that she could leave before Hewson noticed.

Suspiciousness hovered over his brow. "Where are you going, then?"

"I was going to try and fish in the stream. There's

been talk that people have seen a few fish in the river lately. If we're going to catch any, I thought the morning time might be the best."

"We've lived here for two years and have barely seen any fish. Why would there be some now?"

"I don't know." She lifted her arms slightly. "But it's worth a try, isn't it?"

"I'll go with you, then. I don't want you going alone." Hewson bent down to pick up his shoes.

Novah internally groaned. Hewson coming along was the last thing she wanted. She was going to have to tell him the truth.

"I'm not going alone. Beck's meeting me there."

His eyes sharpened. "You've been spending a lot of time with Beck the last two weeks."

It was true. Every afternoon for the last two weeks, Novah had snuck away with Beck. It was all pretty harmless. They talked about life before Desolation, growing up in different parts of the country, and compared their favorite music and movies—the regular stuff people would do if the world hadn't collapsed. But Hewson was overprotective. He'd never see her time with Beck as harmless.

"Really?" She feigned ignorance. "I hadn't noticed."

"I don't like it."

"More like you don't like *him*."

"Yeah, okay. I don't like him."

"Why?"

"I don't know. He just rubs me the wrong way."

A stilted laugh slipped out. "That's not a reason. That's a personal opinion."

"I just don't like how he came here, thinking he's all great, and how everybody just falls at his feet—including you. Some of us have worked for the past two years to keep everyone alive, and no one seems to care about that."

"So that's what this is about. Jealousy and a popularity competition?"

"No," he scoffed as if she was being ridiculous. "I also don't like how he's using you."

Beck wasn't using her. If anything, Novah was using him. Even though she'd enjoyed her time with him, their entire relationship was temporary, a means to an end. Novah didn't want to die without experiencing what it felt like to kiss a man. There was something really unfair about that, so she'd get what she wanted from him and then end things. The problem was she hadn't gotten what she wanted. In the two weeks Beck had been at camp, they'd barely even touched. She didn't get it. He seemed interested. He flirted with her, did nice things for her, complimented her, but at the end of the day, he hadn't so much as held her hand.

She inclined her head toward her brother. "You need to relax. Nothing is going on between us. It's just fishing."

Pete, one of the newcomers to camp, approached. He stopped to the side of Hewson, glancing between us as if he could feel how his presence had interrupted their conversation. "The embers from last night's fire went out. What do you want to do?"

"Uh…" Hewson shook his head. He obviously wanted to go fishing with Novah so she wasn't alone with Beck, but his duty to the camp won out. "I'll come check it out."

Oh, thank goodness!

He turned to leave with Pete but paused to give Novah an admonition. "Fishing. That's it. And then no more activities alone together."

She quickly spun around and left. She didn't reply because she had no intention of following his rules until she got what she wanted.

Ever since Novah was little, Hewson had acted like he was more of a father to her than a brother.

Maybe it was time for a little rebellion.

Only a *little*.

Because Hewson was family. He was still the only person alive in the world that Novah could count on.

That was why it was better to say nothing to him than to lie.

Novah

Bomb Shelter in Northeast Wisconsin
Fall 2050 - Nine Years Ago

"Novah, get inside the shelter." Hewson's eyes peeked up at the darkening sky. "There's a storm coming."

"Stop bossing me around. You're not my dad." Novah purposely took two more steps away from the door that led inside the bomb shelter—her personal prison, as she liked to refer to it.

Hewson rushed after her, grabbing her by the arm as if he intended to drag her back inside. "I'll stop bossing you around if you stop being such a brat."

She yanked her arm, trying to free herself from him. "The storm is still a long way away. Why would I go inside right now?"

"What are you, a meteorologist now? You don't know when the storm will be here."

"If it comes fast, I can just run inside." She threw all her strength into pulling away from him and was victorious. She was free. If only for a few more minutes. She used her freedom by running farther away from the shelter. The heavy winds picked up, throwing dead leaves into the air. The added intensity to the moment made her feel daring and strong like she was walking on the edge of a building with a hundred-foot drop below.

"See?" Hewson pointed to the sky. "I told you."

"Oh my gosh, Hewson. It's just a little wind."

"You're so stupid if you think you can outrun these kinds of storms."

"Stop acting like you're the smartest nineteen-year-old that ever lived."

"If I'm still alive, then I think I'm pretty smart—unlike you, who takes risks all the time."

"No one asked you to follow me." She stomped away.

The wind swirled harder, whipping her hair into her eyes and face.

"Novah?" her father called behind her. "It's time to come inside."

Tears stung behind her eyes. She was tired of being locked inside. It had been thirteen days since she'd been let out of the bomb shelter. Severe storms and winds had made it impossible to go outside. All she wanted was a few more minutes where she didn't have to look at the cement walls that caged her in, where she didn't have to listen to the same music over and over, where she didn't have to play Monopoly and Trouble with the other family staying in the shelter with them, or learn how to cut hair from her mom, or pretend like she was so grateful she was still alive.

Sometimes dying seemed like the better option.

"I tried to tell her, Dad, but she won't listen. She's so freaking stubborn!" Hewson yelled that last part as if he wanted to make sure she heard over the thrashing wind.

"Don't you worry about it." Novah glanced over her shoulder just as her dad shuffled Hewson toward the shelter. "I'm the parent. I'll make sure she's safe."

"She probably won't listen to you."

Her dad patted him on the shoulder as he opened the door for Hewson. "I've got this."

The metal door slammed shut before her father

turned around to face her. "I know you don't want to come inside, and I wish things were different. I wish I could let you stay out here, but we can't risk it."

The strong wind gathered together around them, bending what trees were left. Novah stumbled back from the force.

"Novah?" Her dad extended his arm out to her. "Come on, sweetie. It's not safe."

She ran to him, feeling the push of the wind press against her chest. Once by his side, he wrapped his arm around her. "How about I verse you in Rocket League on the PS6?"

"I'll beat you."

"Nah, I'm getting pretty good at that game."

Novah snuggled into him as they walked to the shelter door. "Not as good as me."

Novah

Spring 2058 - A Year and a Half Ago

AFTER A HALF HOUR of seeing nothing, fishing in the river had turned into swimming. The water was freezing, causing a blanket of goosebumps to cover Novah's skin.

Beck sent a splash toward her. "Novah Harper, tell me something about you that nobody else knows."

She flapped her arms out to her side, keeping herself

afloat, which seemed unfair since Beck was tall enough to just stand there.

"I'm amazing at PlayStation."

He smiled in his amused way. "At PlayStation? Like the entire thing? Not just one game?"

"The entire thing." She lifted her chin with confidence. "I can beat you at any game. I had lots of practice playing in the bomb shelter."

"Now, hold up." He swam to where she was, circling her as he talked. "I've played a lot of PlayStation, too... before everything went to crap. I don't think you should be so cocky."

"You wouldn't be able to beat me. I'm, like, crazy good at it."

The corner of his mouth hitched upward. "I guess we'll never know who's better."

"I guess not."

He pushed his body forward, sending a ripple of water into her chest. They were only a few inches apart. Now she couldn't blame her goosebumps on the cold water. Her eyes dropped to his broad shoulders poking out of the water. She wanted to be disgusted with his perfect, freckle-free, golden skin, but she couldn't. Lately, nothing about Beck disgusted her.

Their eyes met, and a rush of feelings collided inside her chest. There was something special in Beck's gaze that made her feel capable but also safe. He continued to stare at her, feeding the flame burning between them.

Then, his eyes dropped to her lips.

Would he kiss her?

Would she let him?

That was the point of all of this, wasn't it?

Most twenty-one-year-olds were long past their first kiss. But spending twelve years living in a bomb shelter had really lowered Novah's chances of becoming an expert at these kinds of activities. She was nervous but knew that her inexperience would be safe with Beck. He was just that kind of guy.

His shoulder moved, but she couldn't see his arm underwater. However, she definitely felt the moment his fingers slowly closed around her waist. His hands were warm against her skin despite the frigid water. It was her turn now. She lifted her arms, wrapping them around his neck. The action moved their bodies closer together, pressing their stomachs against each other.

His head moved to hers—slow, the way time suddenly felt, a crawling pace that was sure to make her racing heart explode. The tips of their noses touched.

Every move was purposeful. Every inch of space he closed between them unhurried, like Beck was savoring the build-up.

Novah closed her eyes and waited.

It took an eternity for his lips to touch hers.

Then, they did.

Lightly, he skimmed the brim of her mouth.

She watched his lips through half-shut eyes as they repeated the motion, gently gliding over hers. The simple friction was nice and had a surprisingly powerful effect.

The kiss had only just begun, but it set off a surge of fire-works down her body. A warm sensation spread through her chest. She wanted more than his careful grazes. She wanted to know what it would feel like to lose herself completely in a kiss.

She closed her eyes and lifted her head to meet his mouth. At the same time, she adjusted her arms so they wrapped fully around his neck. The movement smashed her body against his even more—all subtle signs that she was ready for more.

She pulled Beck closer and pressed her lips deeper into his. The slow way he had approached the kiss was a thing of the past. He matched her intensity with his own raw passion. Chills tickled her arms and neck, then trav-eled down her spine. She felt like she was on fire.

Heat.

So much heat competing with the cold water circling around them.

For the first time in years, surviving wasn't the first thing on Novah's mind. It was Beck—how his chest felt against hers, how his hands moved across her back, the taste of his lips, the feel of his arms wrapped around her. It was glorious, like waking up from the nightmare she'd been living in, only to find paradise.

This one kiss wouldn't be enough to satisfy her. She had opened Pandora's box and wouldn't be able to go back from this moment.

Then, Beck pulled away. She wanted to be disap-pointed, but the giant smile covering his mouth made her heart race *almost* as much as his kiss had. He laughed with that same pure joy that he carried with him. But right now, Novah felt it, too. A smile matching his spread across her lips, and she laughed, too—a giddy, school-girl laugh that made up for all the things Desolation had taken from her.

Joy.

It had been so long since she'd felt that emotion that she almost didn't even recognize it. She could've easily named it something different, a consequence of the kiss, but there was more to it than that. It was Beck and the way *he* made her feel.

And right then, she decided that just because she'd gotten her kiss, things weren't over between them.

Novah wanted more.

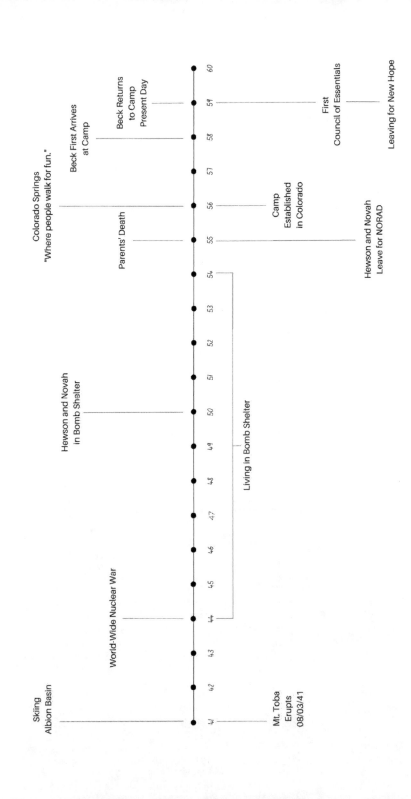

12

Hewson

Summer 2059 - Present Day

The six elected leaders from each camp sat around a broken, uneven table. Hewson had been looking forward to this day for years. They were no longer prisoners to Desolation. The rebuild had begun.

They decided to have their first meeting away from the watching eyes of the three camps, setting up instead in the valley below, next to the make-shift animal pasture. There was a single tree still standing that they used for shade.

"Before we begin," Hewson said, "I think we need to designate a leader among us, like a president of our committee. You know, just to keep order and keep things moving along."

"That's a good idea," Alexis Morris agreed. Alexis was methodical about everything, always looking logically at every situation. She was in her late fifties with mousy brown hair streaked with strands of gray. The corners of her eyes were etched with deep crow's feet that gave her a sense of wisdom. Hewson liked her strong leadership skills from years of serving as a US Senator in Texas. He was glad she was one of the representatives from camp two. She was the only woman among the six leaders elected.

"I'm assuming you want the president to be you?" Andres Gonzales sneered. His black hair swayed as he rattled his head back and forth in annoyance. Andres came to camp with the survivors from Texas, New Mexico, and Arizona. He had a lot of opinions about how things should run. Andres wouldn't have been Hewson's first choice as a representative from camp three, but Hewson didn't live in camp three. It wasn't up to him.

Hewson met Andres's stare. "Yes, I'd like to throw my name in the hat as president."

"I'd like to as well," Alexis said, raising her chin with confidence.

"Anyone else interested?" Hewson looked around the table at the other four leaders. They all shook their heads no.

"Okay, all in favor of Alexis?" Hewson watched as Andres and Marcus Adler, a skinny man with glasses who had originally come from England, raised their hands.

Great. It was going to be a tie.

"And for me?" Danny and Grenham, from Canada, raised their hands.

"Looks like you need a tie-breaker," Beck said, walking into the shade of the tree where they sat.

"What are you doing here?" Hewson spat. "This is a private meeting."

"I want to be added as the seventh elected member."

"It's too late." Hewson dismissed him.

Beck lifted his hand, holding up some papers. "I have three thousand three hundred and forty-six signatures saying it's not too late to add me."

Alexis grabbed the papers out of his hand, looking them over. "He's right. This is a petition for him to be elected as the seventh member of the planning committee." She flipped through each page. "He has the majority of all three camps."

"Well, I say if he has the majority, there's not much we can do." Danny leaned back, chewing on a piece of hay.

"Those papers mean nothing." Hewson bent over, getting his own look at them. "He could've forged those signatures."

"Oh, please!" Andres rolled his eyes. "I watched him collect them in my camp."

"We all know I would've been elected if I had been here." Beck looked around the table. Everyone nodded, and Hewson could feel things shift. They were giving in.

Grenham looked at him, his bald head gathering beads of sweat. "Hewson, it would be nice to have an odd number. Moving forward, we can't keep voting on things and end in a tie."

Why hadn't I thought about a tiebreaker?

Grenham was right. He was a survivor from Winnipeg, Canada. A businessman with a successful past. He liked to get to the point—not waste anyone's time. He had joined camp two years ago with the northern search party. Hewson respected him like he would've his own father.

"Let's vote on it among us," Danny suggested. "Who wants Beck to be added to the group?"

Hewson was the only one who didn't raise his hand.

Great.

Did Beck have to weasel his way into every aspect of his life?

"Well, that settles it." Danny stood, slapping Beck on the back.

"Thanks." Beck smiled. He lifted a bucket around his body and flipped it over, placing it at the table. "I brought my own chair."

"You were that confident we would agree to let you in?" Marcus asked in his thick English accent.

"Of course."

Beck had an air of confidence that made Hewson furious—an entitlement. It had been that way since the first day he came to camp.

"It looks like I'm the tie-breaker between Alexis and Hewson." Beck reached his arm out to her, shaking her hand. "Alexis, you have my vote. Congratulations on being our fearless leader."

Hewson's jaw tightened. How had he lost so much control in a matter of minutes? It was Beck's fault. Everything was always Beck's fault. He didn't think he could hate him any more, but as the meeting started, he realized there was always more room to hate Beck Haslett.

Beck

Summer 2059 - Present Day

"BEFORE WE MOVE FORWARD, we need to decide once and for all who we are," Alexis said.

They'd already spent hours talking circles around each other, but Beck wasn't complaining. This was what he'd wanted, a chance to shape the future for the better. Plus, he'd loved seeing Hewson's furious expression when he'd held up the pages and pages of signatures from people who had wanted him to be included in the planning.

"Are we the United States of America?" Alexis continued. "Rebuilding our country and government system on the foundation of the constitution?"

Marcus from Great Britain scoffed, the wrinkles in his forehead rising together dramatically. "I don't know why we would copy the United States government system." He pushed his glasses back against the bridge of his nose. One side of the spectacles was cracked and broken, but he continued to wear them—probably because he had no other choice. "By 2045, your entire government was corrupt and falling apart. Why do you think the nuclear war started? No, I don't think we want to follow that pattern."

"Now, hold on." Alexis's voice cracked as she spoke. "I take offense to that. The entire government system was not corrupt. I wasn't corrupt. And the *constitution* was not corrupt."

"Marcus, this land here *is* the United States. If you don't like it, you're welcome to return to Europe," Danny said, tipping his cowboy hat toward him.

"I don't know why you're all getting so upset." Marcus shifted nervously in his seat. "It's a moot point. We don't even have a copy of the constitution, unless one of you has the whole thing memorized." He glanced around the table, but nobody answered. "So, we can't copy the previous United States anyway."

"Besides, it *was* the United States, but that country doesn't exist anymore. Nothing does. We have an opportunity to start over with something new and better," Grenham added, taking Marcus's side.

"Of course you would say that," Andres mocked. "You're not even from here, Grenham. You're from Canada. Why don't you go back there and start something new?"

"Why don't you go back to Mexico, where you're from? Aren't you here illegally?" Grenham challenged.

"I'm a citizen of the United States!"

"I bet," Grenham puffed.

Andres swore under his breath as he started to stand, ready to pounce on Grenham.

"Hold it. Hold it." Beck placed a hand on Andres's arm. "Our situation is way too desperate to be fighting about nationalities. Our world has crumbled, and we're not going to get anywhere by fighting. We're on the same team." He looked between the two men. "We've all lost everything in Desolation, and we all need to start over."

Alexis nodded. "Beck's right."

"Maybe we should go around the circle and share our ideas for how we want the new government to be structured," Hewson suggested.

Beck couldn't believe that, for once, Hewson wasn't the one causing the contention.

"For example," Hewson explained, "I like the idea of patterning it after the US with a president who is over everything, and then each state can have local leaders. The camp can be the capital of it all and where the president lives."

Beck was sure Hewson was aiming to be the sole leader of everything and everyone. He was definitely gunning for power.

"Do you still want it to be called the United States of America?" Alexis asked.

Hewson leaned back in his chair. "I don't care what you call it."

"Okay." Alexis made some notes on her paper. "What about you, Marcus?"

"I think we should pattern the area after Europe. Take this land and divide it up into different countries."

"With each country having its own leader and government system?" Alexis leaned forward as if that would help her understand his vision.

"Yes." Marcus nodded. "There are too many opinions. We'll never agree on how things should be run. At least, that way, everyone can make their own government."

Grenham's fingers tapped on the table as he spoke. "I like the idea of the land being divided into different countries, not states. But I think we should all have the same governing laws, at least on a grand level."

"Do you want a single leader who is over all the countries?" Alexis asked.

"No." He shook his head. "As we've seen from the past, one person or group in charge of everything has too much power. Even if there are checks and balances, it eventually goes south. Each country needs its own leader to divide the power, but everyone follows the same government system to promote unity."

Beck liked that idea. He didn't want one person to have complete control over everything, especially if there was a chance that one person would be Hewson.

"Yeah, I don't want one person with too much power, either," Andres added, as if he could read Beck's thoughts. "Each of us could establish a country. We could decide on the laws and rules beforehand so everything is the same."

"Each country would have its own president, then?" Alexis scribbled more notes down on her paper.

"I don't like presidents," Marcus stated flatly. "Kings and queens have ruled successfully throughout history. The use of a monarchy has withstood the test of time more than presidents have."

Danny rubbed his chin as he spoke. "Are you sure about that? Didn't anyone watch *The Crown* years ago on TV? Those people were crazy."

"I'm not talking about *who* they are as people," Marcus explained. "I'm saying that the structure of the monarchical government has lasted long. If you look at the Bible, kings have ruled for thousands of years. It's the very foundation of mankind."

"That's true." Danny nodded.

"If you even believe in the Bible." Andres let out a mocking laugh.

"Fine." Marcus rolled his eyes. "Look at a history book, then."

Alexis bounced her eyes between Danny and Marcus. "So, you're saying you prefer a king instead of a president?"

"It's all just semantics," Grenham said. "They do the same thing."

Alexis furrowed her brows. "Not really. Kings and queens are appointed through blood, not elected. History has shown that a corrupt family line of rulers could be detrimental. Kings and queens have been known to abuse power." She looked at Beck. "What do you think?"

"You have to have elections." Beck leaned back into his chair, folding his arms. "The people have the right to vote on their leaders, and that way, power won't be abused."

"Yes, let's have elections," Hewson said. "But I don't think four years is enough time for a leader to really make his mark. How can any leader get anything done if they are constantly focusing on being reelected?"

Hewson probably wanted to stay in power his entire life.

Marcus shrugged. "Okay, so have an election every twenty or thirty years."

Alexis's eyes went wide. "Thirty years? What if the king or queen is doing a terrible job? Thirty years is too long."

"I like thirty years," Hewson chimed in. "It gives the ruler plenty of time to make plans and carry them out. But I also agree that it could be too long if they are doing a bad job, so we need to put a plan in place where citizens could vote out a king or queen if they were doing a bad job. Like impeachment, except the government doesn't decide. The people do."

Alexis sighed. It was obvious she had difficulty moving away from the United States government system. "I just can't believe you're all leaning toward a monarchy."

"It's a monarchy mixed with a republic," Grenham

explained. "The people still have the power, but we're taking what's good from history, kings, and queens and adding that to what has worked in governments more recently."

It was an interesting plan. Definitely not something Beck saw coming. He would've thought the rebuild would have been patterned after the United States, but as he looked around at the group sitting at the table, he realized how diverse they all were. They were different in race and background. He thought about the survivors in the three camps and the diversity there. Perhaps something different was good—a new kind of government that could unite everyone together. Especially since the most recent way was so divisive.

"So, would these countries be called kingdoms?" Alexis still tried to understand.

"A country or a kingdom. Either way." Marcus shrugged.

The conversation continued on for hours—everyone discussing the pros and cons of the proposed government system. Beck felt anxious. They were only scratching the surface. There were so many details to consider. What if they did something wrong? How would that affect the future of their posterity? The pressure was enormous.

Alexis put down her pencil. "I don't want to vote on this today. I want us all to take the evening and really think about what we discussed. It has been proposed that we divide into seven countries," she added dramatically, "*or kingdoms*, that are ruled by a king or queen. Rulers would be elected every thirty years by the people in their country. Each country would follow and be held to the same laws—the laws that we establish here at camp. If the king or queen does not follow the predetermined laws, or if they are not doing a good job, the people can vote them out of the government at any time."

All eyes glanced at each other. Some people nodded. It wasn't an official vote, but Beck sensed the significance of the moment.

It was the first step to shaping the future.

13

Novah

Summer 2059 - Present Day

"Aking?" Novah's jaw dropped.

She was with Hewson in the pasture, feeding the chickens and horses, but his words had shocked her enough to completely stop what she was doing.

"That's right." The satisfied smile on Hewson's face was proof enough that he was pretty excited by this new development, and this piece of information finally got him to stop complaining about Beck and how he'd ruined the rebuild committee by inserting himself. He'd been stuck on that subject for the past three days. How everything he said or did, Beck said or did the opposite. He swore Beck was only against something because he was for it. Because of the tension between them in the committee meetings, Novah had been extra careful to keep her distance from Beck around camp. She didn't want to add another layer to Hewson's hatred.

"So, someone mentions monarchies, and everyone just says, okay, and then it's done?"

"No." Hewson continued along the fence line. "We talked about the pros and cons of this type of government for days before it came to a final vote."

Novah's brows creased together. "When were you planning on telling me? Or everyone else, for that matter?"

He lifted the bucket in his hand and poured some grain into the next empty food trough. "We're not supposed to discuss what we talk about in our meetings, but it's done now, so I figured I could tell you."

Novah rested her elbow on the fence. "Who voted in favor of a monarchy?"

"Everyone." He started walking again, making her move to catch up.

"*Everyone?*"

She wanted to know what Beck had voted for, but she was smart enough not to come right out and ask.

"Well, everyone except Beck and Alexis."

Beck didn't vote for it.

Something about that made Novah happy.

Hewson must've known what she was up to, because he quickly moved on. "So yeah, I'm going to be a king."

A king?

Novah didn't know how she felt about that, since she

wasn't in the meetings and didn't hear the rationale. The entire thing seemed ridiculous, like some sort of abuse of power.

"I'm not going to bow before you."

"It's not like that. People won't bow before these kinds of kings and queens. It's more of a name than anything else. But I wouldn't stop someone if they wanted to bow." He glanced over his shoulder, throwing her a teasing smile. "And if I'm a king, that would make you a princess."

"That's the dumbest thing I've ever heard," she scoffed. "I'm no princess."

Especially with her hurt foot.

"You are now." He filled up the next bucket.

"The people in camp aren't going to like this when they find out."

"They won't find out until everything is all done and planned. At that point, they'll be so grateful for a plan of action, they won't care *what* the plan is."

"I'm not so sure about that." Novah shook her head. "You better be prepared for a mutiny."

"People crave leadership in whatever form it comes in. They don't want to figure out where to rebuild or how to structure things. They want someone to tell them, to spell it out for them. That's what we're doing. We're planning everything out. Simplifying the process for the majority."

Novah wasn't convinced. "What about other countries? What will they think when they find out the United States no longer exists?"

"Why don't I just call them and see what they think? Or better yet, I could hop on a plane and fly over there." He let out a sardonic laugh. "In case you didn't notice, the entire world got destroyed over the last seventeen years. There are no phones, no planes, no boats. Besides, I don't care what other countries think. I'm sure they're doing the same as us, just trying to survive and rebuild. If they get their crap together first, they can come find us."

Her face tightened. She didn't like Hewson's attitude about the whole thing.

When she didn't respond, he turned to her, seeing the irritation across her face. "Why are you so mad? I thought you'd be happy about the news. Imagine what Mom and Dad would think about all this. I'm going to be a king."

Novah sighed. "I'm just worried that you're doing this for all the wrong reasons. Are you sure the power isn't going to your head?"

"How can you even say that"—Hewson reared back —"when everything I've done in camp the last few years proves otherwise? I've devoted my life to making a home and safe place for the survivors. I've done everything for everyone else. Everything for you!"

"I know." She breathed, feeling guilty for even accusing him of liking the power. "You've been great. I just want to make sure you keep being great."

"I will," he assured. "I'll be the greatest king that ever ruled."

How could Novah refute that?

Hewson had been pushing her for years to keep going. The fact that she was even here and alive was all because of him.

Novah

February 2056 - Three Years Ago

"I KNOW YOU'RE COLD AND TIRED, but we have to keep going." Hewson stood above her curled-up body on the ground.

Debris was everywhere—metal scraps from buildings, shingles from roofs, a lone shoe. It was impossible to get comfortable with the cold and everything pushing into her back. She tucked her arms under her head, using them as a pillow. Her hand felt a drip of moisture. Was it raining? Snowing? She was so hungry she hadn't noticed the rain. Another drip. She opened her eyes to the sky. Not a single cloud. She brushed her fingers against her cheek. The drips were coming from her eyes. When had she started crying?

"Novah, please." Hewson crouched beside her. "We're almost there. I can see the mountains in the distance."

The *far* distance.

Her throat cracked from dryness. "I'm not going. We've walked so many miles. It's too much walking on my bad foot." She closed her eyes, not caring if she died right then and there on the torn-up pieces of concrete. "I'm cold, and my ankle hurts. I'm done."

It wasn't even walking at this point. It was hiking. Hiking over piles of toppled houses and buildings. Her sore foot couldn't take it anymore—protesting, screaming at her with each step forward.

Hewson rubbed his hand on her forehead, pushing her hair back. "I know it hurts." His voice was solemn. "Don't worry. I'll take care of you."

He shuffled around her. He was so loud, banging things, moving things, always searching for stuff to take with us, until he finally snickered.

"Novah?" He rushed toward her. "Look what I found."

She didn't want to open her eyes or even care what he'd found.

He shook her shoulder, begging her to look.

She opened one eye, squinting the other down tighter, forcing out another tear. Hewson bent before her, holding up a green t-shirt.

"What is it?"

His smile was so proud. "Read the logo on the shirt."

She opened both eyes. There was a white silhouette of mountains. Under it, the words *Colorado Springs, Where People Walk for Fun*.

"See?" he said with a grin. "Walking here is fun." He waited patiently for her to laugh.

She didn't know if she had enough energy to laugh, but she did smile...for him. And she knew she would continue walking even if it hurt. She'd do that for Hewson because she owed him that much.

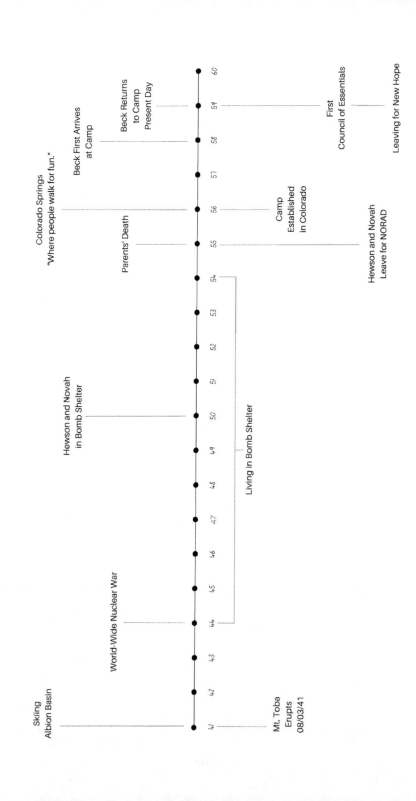

Skiing
Albion Basin

World-Wide Nuclear War

Hewson and Novah
in Bomb Shelter

Colorado Springs
"Where people walk for fun."

Beck First Arrives
at Camp

Beck Returns
to Camp
Present Day

Parents' Death

Mt. Toba
Erupts
08/03/41

41 42 43 44 45 46 47 48 49 50 51 52 53 54 55 56 57 58 59 60

Living in Bomb Shelter

Camp
Established
in Colorado

Hewson and Novah
Leave for NORAD

First
Council of Essentials

Leaving for New Hope

14

Novah

Summer 2059 - Present Day

Novah hadn't talked to Beck since their fake conversation on the couch last week. For Hewson's sake, distance was the best thing—and maybe also for her heart.

Keeping busy was the key to success. She did every extra chore. She picked potatoes and squash in the hot sun. She volunteered to mend everyone's clothes at camp and to cut hair for hours. But there was no more avoiding him now. Beck stood at the entrance of the cave, blocking her exit. The sun was at his back, but there was enough light on his face for her to admire the stubble on his cheeks and how his clothes showed off his toned body.

Novah's eyes darted behind him, checking if Hewson was nearby.

As if reading her mind, Beck motioned over his

shoulder. "He went to camp two to give Grenham something."

Her body relaxed. "Oh."

"Speaking of giving somebody something. I have something for you." He swung his arm around from behind his back, showing three white flowers in his hand. Their heads drooped downward, and their stems were weak and floppy, but the gesture was still cute, even if the flowers were ugly.

Novah had never been given flowers before. It seemed like such a normal thing before Desolation—to give and get flowers—but that wasn't the kind of normal she'd experienced in life. Beck's eyebrows rose as if silently prompting her to take them.

"Thank you." She reached for them. Her fingers brushed up against his, causing a flutter to swirl in her stomach.

"Don't thank me too much. They're dying." His mouth widened into a smile. "I picked them about a mile away."

Novah loved how Beck's eyes sparkled when he talked, as if his happiness could somehow rub off onto her. It used to before she pushed him out of her life.

"Do you know what the worst part about getting flowers during Desolation is?"

"What?" Her brows creased.

"There's nothing you can do with them. It's not like you can go put them in some water. You just have to wait until I leave to chuck them on the ground so I don't see."

Novah laughed, but she definitely wasn't throwing these flowers out. As soon as he walked away, she planned to put them inside her notebook to keep forever next to the picture of her parents.

"You've been busy lately." He'd obviously noticed her work ethic at camp the last week. Did he also know she kept busy to stay away from him?

"What about you? Have you been busy?" It was a stupid question. She already knew exactly what he'd been up to.

He bobbed his head back and forth. "Not too busy, you know. Just deciding the fate of everyone's future. No big deal." The playful sarcasm in his voice brought out her smile.

"Hewson told me a little bit about your meetings. From the sound of things, I should start calling you *Your Majesty*."

"Please don't." A laugh erupted from his throat. "It's surreal the direction things are going, and I can't talk to anyone about it. It's against the rules." He raised his eyebrows. "But it sounds like Hewson's been talking to you. He's going to get in trouble for that."

She brushed his words off. "We tell each other everything."

Beck's glimmering eyes faltered, but he masked whatever he felt and shoved his hands into his pockets. "So, what do you think about what's been decided on? Kings and kingdoms?"

"What do *I* think?" She pointed to herself, taken aback by his question.

"Yes, I'm *dying* to know your opinion. I've wondered for days what you would think about all of this."

Hewson always did the talking, not ever caring about her opinion, so this was a nice change.

"Um...I think kingdoms and monarchs are foreign and archaic. I wonder if everyone, including Hewson, likes the idea of being a king because it seems more powerful and important than being a president." Maybe her opinion was too bold, but Beck's smile encouraged her to keep going. "Do all of the leaders just want prestige?"

"Probably." He shrugged. "But then I wonder if this is how the future is supposed to be. Like, maybe God planted these ideas into our minds, directing us."

"Wow. Did you just go there?" she snickered.

"I did." He grimaced. "I went to religion."

"You better be careful," she teased, "or you might end up offending half the survivors at camp."

"Does that include you?"

She sucked in a breath. "I'm still undecided about God. It's almost easier to believe that He doesn't exist than to believe that He does and that He let the world get destroyed."

"I can see that." Beck nodded. "But it's different for me. And I could be wrong for believing this way, but I like feeling like I'm a part of something bigger. Like I survived *because* God has something special for me to do. I want to believe that I can make a difference."

"You can make a difference, Beck."

"Do I make a difference for you?"

Novah bit the side of her cheek, glancing down.

"Motion to strike that question from the record." The teasing in his voice prompted her to look up.

"Motion granted."

Beck smiled before continuing. "I guess what I'm trying to say is that I can't deny the innate feelings inside me, like I survived Desolation for a reason bigger than me." His eyes darted to hers, and he let out a self-conscience laugh. "Does that make me sound crazy?"

Novah didn't believe the same as him. She couldn't see the bigger picture or fathom the possibility of innate purposes. But Beck's hope and optimism about who he was and what he was meant to be was endearing.

"You don't sound crazy. You sound charming with all of your idealism and plans."

His smile widened. "Charming, huh?"

"Shut up." She rolled her eyes, holding back her smile. "What I mean is that you're like the Christopher Columbus or George Washington of our day. You're the somebody in history that everyone will talk about years from now."

"I don't care about being the somebody in history." He took a step forward. "But I do care about being somebody to you."

He *was* somebody to her. But everything surrounding Novah's feelings for him was complicated.

He didn't wait for her response, probably because he knew he wouldn't get one. "Really, I'm just a regular person doing the best I can with what I have to work with. I don't want to make a bad decision or vote for the wrong thing. One wrong move now could lead to something disastrous in two hundred years. It's a lot of pressure."

"I'm sure it is. Maybe you can fall back on your belief that you were meant to be in this position. You're a good leader and an even better guy. If anyone is going to make something good out of all of this misery, it's you."

"Thanks for believing in me." His lips lifted. "Yours is the only opinion that matters to me."

"Well"—she gave him a half-smile—"I meant every word."

"But now I feel stupid." He glanced down, kicking the dirt with his toe. "If you weren't avoiding me before, you will now after my faith talk and my insecurities about making the wrong choices."

"For the record, I wasn't avoiding you." She tried to lie.

"Yes, you were."

"No, I wasn't. I was just busy." It was a solid alibi.

"You. Were. Avoiding. Me." He said each word slowly, trying to make his point.

"Fine." Novah folded her arms across her chest, smiling. "I was avoiding you."

"Am I that bad?" The corner of his mouth curled upward. "I don't look like a lumberjack anymore. That has to count for something."

"It counts a little." She smirked.

More like it counts *a lot*. She didn't know how he managed to do it, but Beck got more handsome every day, just adding to her complicated feelings.

"Excuse us." Two men carrying a ripped king mattress stood behind Beck. The men took a few steps inside the cave. "This was just recovered in the wreckage, so we thought we'd bring it in here for people to sleep on."

Novah pressed her back against the cave wall, allowing the men to get past.

"Do you need some help?" Beck asked.

"No, I think we've got it."

Beck moved out of their way, too, shifting so he faced Novah. His chest and hips lightly pressed against hers, and he looked down at her with an impish smile. "Pardon me." His warm breath tickled her skin, sending a pulse of attraction through her body.

It had been so long since they'd touched like this. She'd almost forgotten the power his closeness had over her. She wanted to reciprocate the way she used to, but instead, she slid her hands behind her back, feeling the cold rock wall. His heated stare swept over her face and landed on her lips, bubbling more attraction to the surface, like a volcano ready to blow.

The rush of excitement made her heart beat wildly in

her throat and all the way up to her ears. If she stood there any longer, her resolve would soften, and she'd end up dragging Beck's lips down to hers like some kind of kissing monster.

"I think the coast is clear now," she said.

"Is it?" Beck's lips danced with playfulness as he smirked back at her. "I hadn't noticed."

She nudged her hips into him, pushing his body back from hers until she could side-step away from him and exit the cave.

"Hey!" he called. She glanced over her shoulder back to him. "Don't get so busy again that you forget about me."

Novah smiled.

She couldn't forget about Beck even when she tried.

At that very moment, her mind flipped to memories of the past, recalling—*in great detail*—what it felt like to kiss Beck Haslett.

She'd had a lot of practice getting those details just right.

15

Beck

Spring 2058 - A Year and a Half Ago

The tip of Beck's nose brushed against Novah's as they lay in the dirt by the river. They'd spent the last hour making the most of their alone time—which meant kissing more than talking. The perfect way to spend an afternoon, if Beck had any say in it.

He'd only been at camp for one month, but it was the best month of his life. Even if Desolation hadn't happened, he'd still count the last few weeks with Novah as his best moments.

He loved her.

Yeah, it was probably too fast to feel that much, but he didn't care.

Beck loved Novah, and there was no point in denying it.

However…he wasn't stupid enough to say that to her.

153

In fact, he didn't say anything about their relationship to her at all. He didn't want to push too hard too soon. Plus, he had Hewson to worry about. As far as older brothers went, Hewson was the most overprotective jerk he'd ever seen. Beck doubted that anyone would be good enough for Novah in her brother's eyes. They'd spent the last month sneaking around so that Hewson didn't find out about them. Beck didn't complain at first. The sneaking added another layer of excitement to their relationship that made everything more exhilarating. But now that his feelings had progressed, he wanted the whole thing with Novah.

Beck wanted the future.

His head slowly tilted toward her as his lips skidded across hers.

Slowly.

Scarcely.

But it only took a few seconds before desire took the lead. Novah turned her body toward him, draping her leg across his. The kiss went on and on with more passion than before. Beck knew if he let things continue, neither one of them would be strong enough to stop, and although he wanted to be with Novah completely, he didn't want it to happen this way, when they were sneaking around and hiding their relationship. He wanted it to be special, something that forged their commitment together.

He pulled his head back, but Novah's lips followed after him.

"We better stop," he whispered.

"Why?" She kissed his cheek and down along the side of his face to his neck.

"You know why." He closed his eyes, trying to stay strong despite her temptations.

"Come on," she said between kisses. "Post-Desolation girls like me have a lot of catching up to do. And right now, I'm making up for lost time."

"Let's play a game instead." Beck sat up, moving his hands to his own lap.

"A game?" Novah groaned behind him. "I doubt it will be more fun than what we're already doing."

"Yeah, a game." He turned over his shoulder, smiling down at her.

Her brown hair fell out of her ponytail in places—probably from the way they'd been making out for the last hour. The sun shone through the trees, highlighting her face. Her eyebrows—somehow shades darker than her light-brown hair—accentuated the yellow flecks on the outer ring of her brown eyes. She looked so beautiful that it hurt. But Beck couldn't dwell on that right now, or he'd lie back down and continue where they'd left off.

"Okay." She sighed, conceding. She sat up, too. "What kind of a game?"

"It's called *What Do You Miss the Most?* You have to say one thing you miss from before Desolation, and then it's my turn." He hoped she could tell by the playful tone in his voice that he didn't want anything serious, like family members. Everyone missed their families. There wasn't any point saying it out loud.

A smile crept onto her lips. "Top of my list has to be cinnamon rolls."

"Cinnamon rolls?" He raised a questioning eyebrow. "More than toilet paper or showers or toothpaste?"

She shrugged, leaning back against the palms of her hand. "My mind always goes directly to food. I can't help it."

Beck didn't blame her. His mind wandered to food a lot, too. "Let's do two separate games. One for food and one for things we miss."

"Okay, let's start with *things*." She squinted her eyes as she weighed her options. "I would have to say—"

"Chips and salsa," he interrupted.

Her brows furrowed in confusion. "I thought we weren't doing food."

"We're not. I just needed to get that off my chest. We couldn't have cinnamon rolls out there alone."

Her smile grew. He hoped it was because of him, not the mention of chips and salsa.

She stared at the river in front of her. "You make a good point about toilet paper, but I'm going to take it a step further." She turned her head, narrowing her eyes in on him. "Tampons. I miss tampons even though I never had the chance to use them. But I imagine they'd be pretty incredible."

Beck tried to hide the horror he felt.

"What?" She giggled. "Can't you handle it?"

"Oh, I'm handling it. I didn't even flinch when you said tampons."

"The look on your face suggests otherwise."

Beck pointed to himself dramatically. "No, I'm a mature man. A man who can talk about tampons."

"It's part of the basics."

"Let's talk about them." Beck cleared his throat. "*Tampons.* I can see how you would wish you had them. You need them when—"

"Stop!" she said in between laughs, nudging his shoulder with hers. "I do not want to talk about tampons with you."

"So, *you're* not mature, then." He added fake seriousness to his words.

She shook her head, still grinning. "No, I guess not."

"Okay, let it be known," his voice got louder as if he was telling everyone around them, even though there was no one there, "I'm the mature one here. I can talk about tampons all day if need be."

"Move on," she groaned.

"What? You brought it up."

"And now I am *un*bringing it up."

"Fine. It's my turn, then." Beck took a deep breath. "What about toenail clippers?" He sat back, satisfied with his answer.

"Toenail clippers?" she scoffed. "That's a terrible answer!"

"What? Why? Haven't you ever had an ingrown toenail? Nothing hurts more than those. Especially when you try to put your jeans on and your toe hits the side of your pants. It's got to be worse than child labor."

"Toenail clippers are more of a luxury than a *need*. You can rip off your nails out here if you need to. Clippers aren't essential to survival."

"And tampons are?"

She thought about it. "No, not really. I guess that's the big question. What's essential to survival?"

Beck's eyes swept over her face.

Novah was essential to his survival.

16

Beck

Summer 2059 - Present Day

Everyone talked over each other during the planning meeting. Alexis tried to tell the group the need for something similar to the Constitution of the United States—a document that established the fundamental laws of all seven kingdoms moving forward. Marcus opposed anything patterned after the US government. Grenham argued that we didn't need to spell out laws for everybody, that we were so far off from anything like that. For now, he wanted people just to use common decency. Danny and Hewson didn't want to talk about laws yet. They both thought laws should be discussed last, when everything else was planned out. They wanted to split up the land first.

Beck didn't comment. Instead, he listened to everyone's point of view, letting it all sink in. Listening to the ideas seemed like the best course of action. He'd take the best of what each of them said and propose a plan considering all of that.

But after a while, listening to everyone fight gave him a headache. He let his mind drift to Novah. To the waves of natural curl that framed her face when the rest of her brown hair was mostly straight. She probably wished the natural waves weren't there, but Beck loved them. Each curl was touched with golden highlights from the sun. He also loved the smattering of dark-brown freckles on her nose and cheeks. Once, he'd even played dot to dot on her cheekbones while her body giggled below him.

"You guys are all missing the point," Hewson said, breaking him from his thoughts. "We need to figure out the basics first."

The basics.

Novah liked talking about the *basics.* Beck inwardly laughed, thinking back to when things were still easy between them, when they spent hours together, kissing and talking and then kissing some more.

That was when a memory popped into his head.

A *specific* memory.

Beck straightened in his chair as the heated conversation continued around him. "What is essential to survival?" he said out loud.

"What?" Hewson asked, irritated by the interruption.

Beck spoke up. "What is *essential* to our survival? Essential to have in a rebuild? That's what we should be focusing on, the essentials."

The group eyed each other quietly until Alexis finally replied, "I like that. The essentials," she repeated. "Our role is to council together, deciding what is essential for the future."

Beck added, "Not necessarily what is essential in the distant future, but right now. What is essential right now?"

"Everything is essential right now," Hewson balked. "We have nothing."

"You're right. We have nothing," Grenham said. "But that's why everything *can't* be essential. We have to pick and choose what we can actually do in a rebuild. Resources are scarce. Manpower is scarce. We can't plan a future based on what we were used to in the past. We have to start from scratch."

"Focus only on the things we really need?" Marcus said it like a question. "When other countries built their governments, they already had the essential things figured out. Food, clothing, housing, water. We don't have any of that in place on a large scale."

"If something isn't essential to survival, then we ditch it. If we decide that it is essential to the rebuild, then we figure out a way to make it happen." Beck looked at everyone around the table. "As we start to make our list of what is essential, the rest will fall into place because we'll know what things to focus on."

Alexis smiled for the first time all afternoon. "Yes. We're not leaders planning a rebuild. We are The Council of Essentials."

The Council of Essentials.

Beck liked that.

He especially liked how it was inspired by Novah.

Hewson

THE COUNCIL OF ESSENTIALS.

Hewson liked the idea but hated that it came from Beck.

This was exactly what he was afraid of. He was the one that was supposed to be shaping the rebuild. Not Beck. But everyone seemed more interested in listening to Beck's ideas than his own.

He needed to take control of this meeting before he lost all say completely.

"There are seven of us." Hewson pointed at every leader around the table with the tip of the small rock in his hand. "The way I see it, we need to divide what is left of the continent into seven countries." Hewson drew an outline of North America on the table in the middle of the group. The chalky rock made scratching sounds against the wood table as he pressed.

This was the fun part—dividing up the land.

"*Kingdoms*." Marcus smirked.

"Okay, kingdoms, if you prefer to call it that."

"But we don't really know what is left of the continent," Danny said. "After all the destruction, the land might be different."

"We have a pretty good idea." Beck leaned over the

chalk drawing, pointing to Oregon and Washington. "The first big earthquakes, the ones in 2045, were in this area. They hit the northwest part of the country, Seattle, Portland—"

"And Vancouver," Grenham cut in.

"Yes, all that area was completely destroyed," Beck said. "Those cities fell into the earth. Anything that was left was wiped away by the tsunamis that followed."

"So, we know that land isn't an option anymore." Hewson crossed out the left corner of the map.

"You might as well cross out California and where the Baja used to be." Beck pointed to that part of the map. "We know from the few California survivors that all of that area is underwater and flooded. We shouldn't try to go past the Sierra Nevada mountains." Then, he pointed at the other side of the map. "Same thing with the East Coast. It's all underwater."

Here we go again, with Beck taking over the conversation.

But Hewson drew X's over every state along the coast anyway. "Let's just assume that everywhere that used to border water is flooded now, creating new coastlines that are more inland."

"Camp is roughly here." Marcus pointed to the center of the drawing, where he thought Colorado might be. "I don't think we want to travel too far north into Canada or too far south into Central America. For now, we should all stay fairly close to where we started. Especially since travel is difficult."

"I agree," Andres nodded. "There's not enough of us to scatter everywhere just yet."

"Actually, I want to take a group north, back to where Canada was. Not too far. Just to Calgary or Edmonton at the most," Grenham said.

Hewson drew some lines in the north, staking out where Grenham wanted to be. "If you're willing to go up that far, I guess it's okay. Does anybody else have any requests?"

"I do." Andres raised his hand. "I want the south where it's warm. Where Arizona, New Mexico, and Texas bordered Mexico."

Hewson marked that area off for Andres. Then, he looked up at the group. "Personally, I'd like to stay here in Colorado. I did establish the first camp, and I've been here the longest out of all of us."

"How convenient for you," Beck muttered. "You already have temporary water, shelter, and crops."

"I think I've earned that convenience."

"And we haven't?" Beck challenged. "I left camp for a year to go look for survivors."

Hewson's body tensed. "That was your choice. But I was needed here."

"You *think* you were needed here, but I'm sure people could've gotten along just fine without you."

Alexis looked back and forth between the two of them. "Okay, let's move on before the two of you rip each other's heads off. I'm fine with Hewson staying here. Does anybody else, besides Beck"—she gave him a pointed look—"have any problems with that?"

"I don't have a problem with it." Beck lifted his shoulders. "I expected Hewson to take the easy way out."

"Well, it's better for my sister with her ankle if we don't go somewhere far." His words held a lot. It was his not-so-subtle way of warning Beck not to get any ideas about convincing Novah to go with him wherever he ended up.

"It's fine." Danny jumped in, putting a hand on Beck's arm as if to keep him from reacting.

"I'm okay with it, too." Marcus nodded.

"I'd like to go north as well," Danny said. "Wyoming and into Montana where my ranch was. I want to get back there and see what's left after all the volcanic activity in Yellowstone National Park. I also buried a time capsule with my wife of special things that I'd like to dig up."

"You can have it. I wouldn't touch Yellowstone with a ten-foot pole." Hewson marked off the land below Grenham for Danny.

Alexis looked at Beck and Marcus. "That just leaves us three."

"I don't care where I go," Marcus stated. "It's all a hellhole. You guys choose."

"Well, if nobody minds, I'd like a shot at the south. Atlanta, Alabama, etc… I grew up there." She looked at Beck. "But I get if you want that area since you're from North Carolina."

"There's nothing left for me there." He leaned forward, pointing to the map. "I'll take the west."

Marcus laughed. "Good, because I really didn't want to cross the Rocky Mountains to get out west."

"I'm up to the challenge," Beck said, looking right at Hewson, implying that he wasn't up for a challenge, even though everything Hewson had done—trekking to Colorado with his sister's bad foot, setting up the camp, running the camp—proved otherwise.

He swallowed back his anger. This wasn't the time to let Beck have it. There would be other moments to give him what he deserved. "Marcus, that leaves you what's left of Wisconsin, Missouri, Iowa, South Dakota." Hewson drew a kidney-shaped oval over that area.

"Sounds great," Marcus said. "Although, we'll probably steer clear of St. Louis for now."

The group nodded, looking over the map and the lines that marked the seven new kingdoms. It was a rough sketch, but Hewson knew exact boundary lines weren't really necessary at this point. All that mattered was that they divided the land.

"That went better than I thought it would." Alexis clapped her hands together in excitement. "Does anybody know yet what they want to call their new kingdom?"

Marcus leaned forward, putting his forearms on the circular table. "We should name them now so we don't keep referring to the old names. Let's move forward the way we intend to."

"It seems like kind of a big deal. Maybe we should take a day to think about it," Beck suggested.

Hewson rolled his eyes. Why hadn't Beck already started thinking about what he'd name his kingdom? They'd known for a week about this.

"I think everyone makes too big of a deal out of it. Let's not overcomplicate this." Grenham slapped the table in front of him. "Northland. My kingdom will be called Northland."

"I'm going to name my kingdom after my daughter, Enderlin." Danny's eyes clouded over with moisture. "She didn't survive Desolation, but now her memory can live on forever."

"Tolsten," Marcus spat. "I want my kingdom to be called Tolsten. It was the name of the street I grew up on. A lot of happy memories there."

"Okay," Alexis said, writing it down. "I love the Appalachian Mountains. I'd love to settle at the foot of them if they still exist, so I'll call my kingdom Appa."

"Cristole. After my wife." Andres's words were quiet.

Everyone nodded and then looked at Beck as if it were his turn next. He scratched his arm as he thought, then he let out a deep breath. "New Hope. The kingdom of New Hope."

Hewson had to choke back a laugh. It was so cliche, but that was Beck, always bringing in faith and hope.

"My kingdom will be called Albion," Hewson finally said, offering no explanation. He masked the flickering emotion inside him. He wasn't about to tell anyone that he was naming his kingdom after his favorite memory with his father.

Alexis finished writing down the last few names, then she dropped her pencil, clasping her hands together. "All of your names are lovely. I think the future looks bright for these seven kingdoms. Their potential is endless."

Hewson

Spring 2041 - Seventeen Years Ago

"YOU SHREDDED THAT SLOPE," Christian Harper said as he tugged his ski goggles down. "I think that's the best I've ever seen you ski."

"I'm still not as good as you." Hewson looked up at his dad. A few beads of sweat gathered at the base of his brown hair.

"You're better than I am, or at least you will be. Just give it a couple of years."

Hewson couldn't help but smile. Better than his dad someday? That seemed crazy. His dad was the best at everything, especially skiing.

Christian squinted up at the sun. "We still have a couple of hours left. What do you want to do? Get lunch or keep skiing?"

"Definitely keep skiing."

"That's what I was hoping you'd say." He ruffled

Hewson's hair. "It's your weekend, pal. We'll do whatever you want to do."

This entire trip had been about Hewson. He and his father had spent weeks planning it. Poring over the computer, researching ski resorts. They settled on Utah. Skiing the slopes in the beautiful Albion Basin. Just the two of them.

"What slope do you want to do next?" his dad asked.

"Let's take the high-speed quad lift to the top of Albion Basin. Then, we can decide what hill to ski down from there."

"Sounds like a plan. To the top of Albion!" his father playfully shouted, pointing his ski pole at the snow-packed mountain towering over them.

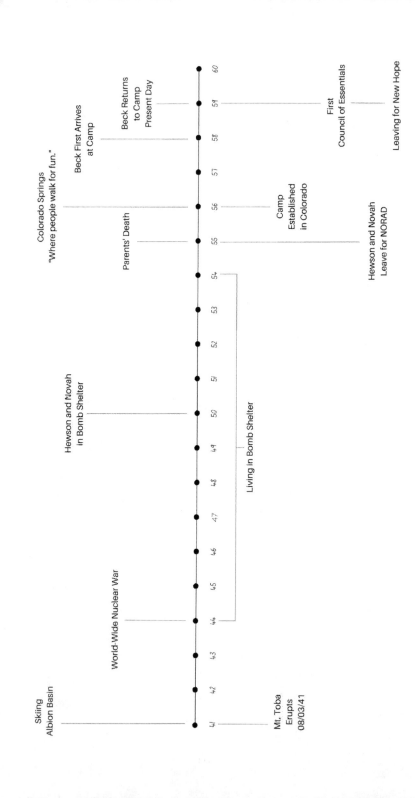

Skiing
Albion Basin

Colorado Springs
"Where people walk for fun."

Beck First Arrives
at Camp

Beck Returns
to Camp
Present Day

Hewson and Novah
in Bomb Shelter

Parents' Death

World-Wide Nuclear War

First
Council of Essentials

Leaving for New Hope

Camp
Established
in Colorado

Hewson and Novah
Leave for NORAD

Living in Bomb Shelter

Mt. Toba
Erupts
08/03/41

41 42 43 44 45 46 47 48 49 50 51 52 53 54 55 56 57 58 59 60

Beck

Summer 2059 - Present Day

"Is this seat taken?" Aycee asked at dinner, nodding to the stump next to where Beck sat. The camp buzzed with chatter and excitement as everyone discussed the information the committee had announced today. They'd been discussing things every day for the past four weeks, and it was finally time to let the camps in on some of the preliminary plans.

"Uh, no." Beck stood, gesturing for Aycee to sit in the more comfortable chair he was in. "But take this seat instead."

"Aww, you're such a gentleman." Aycee smiled at him before lowering into the twisted camp chair.

His eyes swung to Novah before sitting down on the stump, but she was already looking at them from across the fire.

"What an exciting day!" Aycee's bubbly voice caught him off guard for a second. "It was so much fun finally hearing bits and pieces about the rebuild plans. I mean, kings and queens and new countries. It's all so romantic."

"Not everyone feels the way you do."

The nagging feeling in his chest expanded with his lungs as he drew in a breath. He looked at the group of people arguing with Hewson and Danny the next fire over.

Aycee followed his stare. "Oh, those people will get over it. If they wanted something different, then they should've tried harder to be on the rebuild committee."

Beck shrugged. "I just hate feeling like I let people down."

"Oh, my gosh. You could never let anyone down. Especially me." Aycee flipped his concerns away just as easily as she'd flipped her auburn hair behind her shoulder. "I'm so excited to finally think about the future after all the difficulty we've been through."

Beck's eyes shot to Novah again, missing how his conversations with her went. He could share his pressures and concerns, and she'd validate them, unlike Aycee, who dismissed everything so easily. It wasn't Aycee's fault. She was a dreamer, a lot like himself. But he craved something different to balance him out, pull him down from the clouds when his dreams got too big, and push him back up when he was meant to be great.

"I love that you named your kingdom New Hope." Aycee leaned in, rubbing the side of Beck's shoulder.

"There's just so much positivity behind that name. It's pretty straightforward, but is there a story to how you came up with it?"

"Um…" Her touch surprised him, and he tensed, wishing he could roll his shoulder and roll Aycee's hand right off of him. "It's kind of personal."

His eyes flicked to Novah again. Her glare was focused on Aycee, and something about that made Beck smile.

She squeezed his shoulder. "Well, I trust you completely with my future, and New Hope sounds like the perfect utopia to live in."

"I hope so." Beck stood, acting like he was going to clear his dinner plate, but really, he just wanted to get out from under Aycee's impromptu massage. "It was nice talking to you."

She smiled up at him with her dimple. "You, too. Hopefully, we can do it again sometime."

Beck nodded, then walked away. The poor girl was obviously interested in him. He wracked his brain, trying to remember if he'd ever accidentally given her a sign that he was open to something like that. He didn't see how he could've when he'd been hopelessly in love with Novah for the past year and a half. But Aycee was new here. She wouldn't know about Beck and Novah's history.

He walked over to the edge of the camp, where things were darker. His head fell back, and he looked up at the stars twinkling in the night sky. They were the one consistent thing he could count on through Desolation. Everything else about Earth had changed—the weather, the seasons, the landscape, the ocean—but the stars remained.

"Hi."

He smiled, recognizing Novah's voice. It was the first time in the month that he'd been back that she'd sought him out. Usually, it was the other way around. His focus fell on her. "How did you escape your brother's watchful eye?"

"He's so caught up convincing everyone why kings and queens are necessary. He didn't even notice that I left." She flipped her head back, looking at the stars, too. "It's pretty amazing, isn't it?"

"I was just thinking about how everything else has changed, but somehow the stars stayed the same."

"That's true."

They stood in silence for a minute, taking in the brilliant lights.

"What were you and Aycee talking about?" She kept her focus on the sky, avoiding his gaze.

"I knew you were jealous." Amusement played across his expression.

"What?" Novah's brows creased together. "No, I wasn't."

"Then, why do you want to know?"

She eyed him, biting the side of her cheek. "Okay, fine. I was a little jealous."

It was the best admission he'd ever heard, and he laughed.

That was when Novah punched him in the shoulder. "Oh, don't be so happy about it."

"I'm sorry. It's just...I've never seen you jealous before. It's totally cute."

"It's ridiculous." She looked at him. "I know that."

"Well, you can rest easy. She just wanted to talk about today's announcement and why I named my kingdom New Hope."

"Did she need her hand on your shoulder to talk about all of that?"

Beck laughed harder. "It was a very intimate conversation."

She playfully punched him again, which was the best feeling in the world. Their relationship was still thin and breakable, but he felt the shift—the falling of another one of her walls.

"Do you know why I named my kingdom New Hope?"

"Because you wanted to inspire hope for your country's future?"

Beck smiled. "Well, yes, but that's not the only reason."

"Then why?" She looked up at him with her brown eyes.

"I named it after you."

"Me?"

"You once told me Novah means *new*. So really, my country means *hope for you*."

"You shouldn't have—"

"If you want, I can name it after Aycee."

"No, that's okay." Her spine straightened, clearly not liking that idea. "Thank you. I've never had a kingdom named after me."

His head tilted toward the sky. "People used to have stars and galaxies named after the ones they loved. But not me. I name kingdoms."

He'd casually thrown the word *love* in there just as a reminder. It wasn't the first time he'd said it to her, but he wanted her to know that his feelings hadn't changed.

Her gaze held his. "It's a really nice gesture."

Was his love the nice gesture or naming the kingdom after her? He hoped the kingdom naming. But either way, Beck wasn't going to complain. This casual drop of his feelings went better than the first time he'd told her he loved her.

18

Novah

Beginning of Summer 2058 - A Little Over a Year Ago

"Congratulations!" Danny slapped Benji on the back. "Way to make something good come out of Desolation."

Benji squeezed Samone's shoulder. "I'm just glad she said yes."

Samone smiled, glancing down at the ring on her finger. It wasn't a diamond ring; it was just a simple silver band. Something that had probably come from a cheap jewelry store before Desolation, but Benji had bartered and traded just about everything he owned so that Samone could have an engagement ring.

Novah couldn't stay at camp and watch the happy couple anymore.

She couldn't breathe.

How could she breathe when it felt like she was

drowning in sorrow? She hurried up the path—as much as her foot would let her. When she got to the stream, she turned left into the thick trees, trying to find a safe place to fall apart. She pressed her back against a tree and sank to the ground. Her tears were coming fast and heavy, and her chest heaved, trying to keep up with her sporadic breaths between sobs. She lifted her arm, wiping her tears on her flannel shirt.

She would never have what Benji and Samone have.

She would never stand hand and hand with the man she loved, smiling big, and tell everyone how he proposed. That sort of thing wasn't in the cards for her. And until now, she didn't know how much she wished it was.

"Novah?" Beck's voice was quiet and soft, but she still jumped in alarm. "Are you okay?"

She turned her head away, using her sleeve to wipe at her face again. "I'm fine." She tried to make her voice sound normal, but her emotion betrayed her.

Beck slowly walked toward where she sat. "Can I sit with you?"

She didn't want Beck to see her like this. Their relationship was just physical. She didn't need him to see her mourn the loss of what could never be hers.

"I'm fine. I was actually going to go back." She moved to stand, but her stupid ankle slowed her down.

Beck grabbed her hand, gently tugging her back to her seat against the tree, leaning against it himself. "What's wrong?"

She shook her head, trying to gain some composure. "It's stupid."

"I love stupid."

He felt so safe. His presence alone numbed her pain.

She played with the buttons on her shirt. That was easier than looking at him as she spoke. "I have this memory from when I was a little girl. I was out shopping with my mom. We'd bought way too much, and my mom's hands were full of bags." She let the happiness of the moment wash over her. "My mom was in a hurry to get home to make dinner, but when we came out of the store, my mom stopped. There, in the middle of the courtyard, by a fountain, was a couple getting engaged. We stood and watched as this guy said how much he loved this girl. He got down on one knee, opened a box with a shiny ring, and asked her to marry him." Her mouth moved into a thoughtful smile. "The girl screamed yes, just once, and then threw herself into the boy's arms. I'll never forget what my mom said." Novah's eyes drifted to the ground, lost in the memory. "She said, 'I hope your proposal is one of the greatest moments in your life. When the man who loves you the most in the world asks you to be his, it's magical.'"

She looked at Beck. His legs were stretched out and crossed one over the other. His hands were in his lap. His handsome face searched hers, patiently waiting for her to continue.

"When I saw Benji and Samone, it hit me. I won't

ever have the moment my mom described. Desolation took that from me."

"Who says you can't have that moment? Benji and Samone made it work during Desolation. You can, too."

A bitter laugh vibrated over her lips. "I doubt it."

Beck popped to his feet with a surge of energy. "Hang on."

"What are you doing?" She leaned forward, watching him break off a twig and tie it into a circle to make a ring.

He stepped in front of her, pulling her to her feet. "You're going to think I'm crazy. But don't." He lowered as if he was going to kneel, then quickly stood. "And don't freak out." Then, he dropped to one knee.

Novah's heart pounded uncontrollably. "What are you doing?" It looked like he was proposing. She looked around self-consciously for any spectators, but they were alone.

"I'm giving you your moment." There was enough playfulness in his eyes that she tried to tell herself this was just a joke.

"Beck, this is ridiculous!"

"Would you be quiet?" He smirked. "I'm trying to be romantic."

She knew this wasn't real, but her heart longed to hear what Beck would say if he proposed. She clamped her mouth shut, letting him grab her hand, interlocking his fingers with hers. His hazel eyes gazed into hers.

"Novah, I've known ever since I met you that you

are special, that there is something about you that balances me out. You make me want to be a better man and create a better world just so you can live in it. I've always believed that love is the answer to everything, like why we survived Desolation and why we're here. Novah, you're my answer. You and I are meant for each other. We both survived the craziness of the last seventeen years so we could create an epic love story. I survived all those hard things so I could love you."

He loved her?

Novah's free hand went to her chest as if it could somehow stop her heart from bursting open. Her other hand nervously squeezed Beck's fingers.

"Your dreams about the future are real, and they don't have to stop because of Desolation. I promise you, I'll make them all come true if you'll let me." Beck's eyes pleaded with her. "Let me marry you. Let me love you."

The playfulness was gone from his eyes. This felt real —at least for her—but she couldn't bring herself to speak.

He let go of her hand and pulled the circular twig he'd just made out of his pocket. He stood and slowly slipped the twig on her ring finger. He gazed into her eyes. All that was left was to seal it with a kiss.

Her hand trembled.

Her eyes blinked back tears.

This wasn't real.

This *couldn't* be real. Because if Beck loved her and *if*

she loved him, then he'd just become another person Desolation would take away from her.

Novah pulled back, shrinking from his grasp. "Very good." She infused her voice with as much casualness as she could muster. "You're really smooth, you know. I think fake proposals are your specialty."

Beck's brows folded, and hurt scattered across his face.

It had been real for him.

But she was too far down this road to turn back. Her survival instinct won out. Keeping Beck an arm's-length away was her last step at self-preservation.

"Yeah, I guess so." Beck stepped back, and Novah hated herself for being so callous.

"Thank you for doing that. I'll treasure it forever." She held up her ring finger. "I bet Hewson's wondering where I am. I better go."

She left Beck standing there alone as fresh tears streamed down her face.

19

Beck

Summer 2059 - Present Day

"Marcus, why don't you start with your list of the most essential things? We'll go around the table, each saying anything new off of our lists that no one else has mentioned, but my guess is, we'll all have similar stuff." Alexis raised her eyebrows eagerly, indicating for Marcus to start.

"Okay," Marcus said, clearing his throat. "Food, water, shelter, fire, warmth, clothing, safety, sun protection, basic furniture." He glanced up. "Maybe a knife and a working bathroom." Everyone laughed at the working bathroom part.

"Perfect." Alexis smiled at Marcus before turning to Hewson. "What about your essential items?"

"I have some of those things plus health, skills, and

knowledge, first aid, sleep, oxygen, money or some kind of way to exchange goods, and safety."

"Good additions," she said, nodding. "Danny, what's on your list?"

"I'd add freedom, peace, self-development, water purification, core values, and purpose to the list."

Alexis shifted her eyes to Beck. He glanced down at his paper. He had most of the items that were mentioned before, but he also had a lot that hadn't been mentioned yet. "Relationships, friends, family, marriage, reproduction—"

"Leave it to Beck to have sex on his list." Andres laughed.

Beck smiled, shaking his head. "No, not sex but a way to repopulate. None of what we're doing matters if we don't repopulate humankind."

Danny wagged his brows. "I think we all can remember the way to repopulate. I know I can."

Beck smiled, hoping his face didn't show how embarrassed he was. He decided to ignore the teasing and continue with his list. "Faith or some sort of spiritual connection with divinity." He heard a few snickers, but that was to be expected. "And top on my list"—he looked right at Hewson—"love."

"Love isn't essential," Hewson disagreed, his eyes like daggers.

It was to Beck.

There was something about Novah that made him

feel like he couldn't live without her. He needed her as much as he needed food, water, and shelter.

"We aren't here to argue anything on anyone's lists." Alexis tried to moderate. "There was a lot of good stuff on there. Thank you, Beck. Does anyone else have anything?" She scanned her own list. "I think everything has been covered on mine."

Grenham raised his hand and then let it rest on his bald head. "I would add infrastructure and travel, as well as animals."

"Oh, yes. Definitely," Alexis said. "Let's start with the most basic stuff: food, water, and shelter. Those items are the most essential things. Once we have those items planned out, we'll move on to the other items on our lists. I'm sure this process will take us several weeks if we want to do it right."

Beck was grateful for the time it would take to sort everything out.

He needed every second he could get to soften Novah.

Because he wasn't leaving for New Hope without her.

She was essential to him.

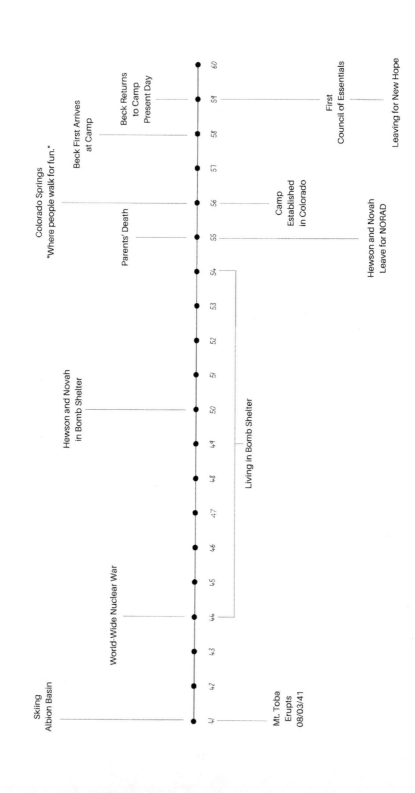

20

Novah

Summer 2059 - Present Day

Novah pushed her knife into a cucumber, trying to keep each slice about the same size, or else someone at camp would inevitably complain that so-and-so got more food for dinner than them.

"You're lucky," Aycee said, working beside her. They'd been standing by each other, cutting vegetables, for ten minutes and hadn't spoken a word to each other. Novah wasn't even sure Aycee was talking to her.

"What?" She eyed her.

"You're lucky." Aycee stopped chopping and turned her body toward her. "You already know what kingdom you're going to live in."

"How?" Novah's brows pinched together in confusion. Had she missed some kingdom-choosing meeting where they divided each survivor into their future country? The ultimate school-yard pick.

"Well, obviously, you'll stay in Albion with Hewson."

"Right." Novah's shoulders dropped, and her focus returned to peeling her next cucumber. "I'm always with Hewson." She couldn't keep the bitterness from her voice.

"I'm hoping to go with Beck to New Hope." There was a little too much giddiness in Aycee's words for Novah's liking. "That's my plan, at least. I mean, he hasn't asked me or anything like that. It's more like wishful thinking on my part."

She forced a reassuring smile, ignoring the stabbing feeling in her chest. "That sounds like a good plan."

Or the worst plan Novah had ever heard.

Until recently, she hadn't pictured Beck with another woman. Her sole focus had been on protecting her heart by pushing him away. But the way her heart broke just thinking about Beck with Aycee made her reconsider everything. What was the worse pain? Giving her whole heart to him and losing him to the elements? Or watching him love someone else? But if they were in New Hope, she wouldn't necessarily have to watch. Maybe what she didn't know wouldn't hurt her.

"I'm not super thrilled about starting over again, but Beck's worth it. He's going to be such a good king. Some people were just born to reign, you know."

Novah nodded. It was better than rolling her eyes. Not that she didn't think Beck would be a good king, but born to reign? That sounded so stupid. She didn't want Hewson to think that about himself, or it would go straight to his already inflated ego.

"You're also lucky that your ankle is hurt," Aycee continued.

Yes, so blessed.

"I'm not looking forward to the walk to New Hope. It's going to be a trek for sure."

A trek Novah wasn't sure she'd be able to make even if she wanted to.

"Hey, ladies," Beck said behind them.

Aycee turned with an animated smile, and Novah felt like taking her knife and cutting her mouth out.

Okay, maybe that was a little dramatic.

And disturbing.

"Hey! We were just talking about you," Aycee said.

His eyes darted to Novah, and his expression lit up. "Really?"

"Yeah, Aycee was saying how she was thinking about moving to New Hope with you." She brought her knife down on the waiting cucumber with a little too much force.

Beck's voice raised in surprise. "I didn't know people were already deciding."

Aycee shrugged. "People are just talking. Weighing their options. Nothing has been decided yet. But the choice has to be made soon."

"I see." He nodded.

"How did the planning meeting go today?" Aycee asked.

"Good. We talked about what things were essential to survival and made some decisions on how we would provide the essentials to people."

"What did you say was essential?" Aycee lifted her shoulder toward him. Her flirting skills were on point, and Novah couldn't help her irritation.

"I said *love* was my most essential item."

Novah's heart blew up, sending a burst of heat to her cheeks. She didn't need to look up to know that Beck's eyes were on her. No doubt, he studied the bright blush painting her face. Even if he stood a football field away, he could see it. She tried to keep her movements normal, but her stupid trembling hands betrayed her. If she wasn't careful, she'd cut off her finger.

"Love?" Aycee sighed next to her. Thank goodness Aycee had an answer. Novah needed the attention *off* of her. "That is so cute. I didn't know you were such a romantic."

"Diehard romantic." Beck casually leaned against the table. His position change put his body a few inches from hers. That was definitely not helping her heart or her flaming cheeks.

"Did everyone agree love was essential to survival?" Aycee asked.

"Not everyone." His head tilted, a clear sign his eyes were on her again. "Hewson thought it was a dumb idea."

"Oh." Aycee turned awkward, probably not sure how to respond since Hewson was Novah's brother. "Well, I'm sure there are a lot of different opinions that you have to weed through."

"Hey, Aycee!" Indie called from over by the fire. "Can you come stir and watch the stew for me? I have to go to the bathroom."

The fire was twenty feet away. Novah was thrilled about the distance.

"Uh, sure." The disappointment in Aycee's voice was easy to pick out. She'd rather stay and talk to Beck, but she set her knife down and reluctantly walked to the fire.

"Thanks." Indie handed her the spoon and walked away but not before she winked back at the two of them.

Beck chuckled. "She's as subtle as a hailstorm."

"Yeah, I've noticed she likes to get us alone."

"I'm not complaining. I was hoping to talk to you."

"We are talking." She smirked.

"I know, but I have something I want to give you." He reached into his pocket and grabbed something. "Close your eyes and hold out your hand."

"Why?" she balked.

"Because it will be fun."

Novah pursed her lips together but obeyed. She held her hand out and closed her eyes. He dropped a small bottle into her palm.

"Okay, open."

Her gaze immediately darted to her hand and to the bottle of ibuprofen that Beck had placed there. Medicine, especially painkillers, was unheard of. They were some of the first things to go when everything went south in the world. Novah hadn't seen anything like this since she lived in the bomb shelter.

"You're joking." She twisted the cap and looked inside, then her wide eyes whipped to him. "It's three-fourths full."

"I know."

"How did…" Her head shook. "Where did you find this?"

"I got it from Cameron in camp two."

"He just *gave* it to you?"

"Well, no." Beck shrugged. "I traded him for it."

"What did you trade?"

"My tarp, tent, purifier…" He hesitated. "And my Swiss Army knife."

"No, Beck!" She gasped. "You didn't! That knife was the last thing you had left from your dad."

"So?"

She handed back the pills. "So, that was too much. I'm not worth it."

He closed her fingers over the bottle, leaving his warm hand on top of hers. "You're worth it to me."

Tears filled her eyes. It was the nicest gesture and sacrifice anyone had ever made for her. She reached for him with her free hand, pulling him into a hug. "Thank you," she said into his neck.

He wrapped his arms around her body. "I'm glad you like it."

They stood there, soaking in each other in the most perfect hug that she'd ever experienced, not caring who in camp watched. The closeness of their bodies and the way their arms held each other conveyed all the things they didn't or *couldn't* say to each other. His hand gently swept down the back of her head, running along her hair. There was a tenderness to everything Beck did that made her feel safe, like Desolation couldn't hurt her anymore. At that moment, her reasons why she'd said they couldn't be together didn't seem important.

Yeah, there was Hewson.

And there was her fear of losing Beck and her inability to handle it.

But the fear of never having him was almost worse.

"Get off my sister!"

Novah jumped, turning to face Hewson's glare.

Of course he would find them hugging.

Hewson's fist clenched as if he considered throwing punches in Beck's direction. It wouldn't be the first time.

"I told you to leave her alone."

"It was just a hug," Beck muttered, backing away.

Hewson's blue eyes blazed with hatred. Novah stepped in front of him, hoping to distract him enough to calm him down. "I was just thanking Beck." She held up the bottle of ibuprofen in front of his face. "Look what he gave me. It's incredible, right?"

Hewson's eyes flipped to Beck. "So, what? You're trying to buy Novah's love now?"

Beck pushed out a stoic laugh. "It's called a gift. If

you ever thought about anyone other than yourself, then you'd know that."

"She doesn't want your gift." His eyes swung to her as if he wanted her to give the medicine bottle back, but instead, she stood silent. "Novah?" he pressed.

Beck looked at her. "You don't have to give it back." He began walking backward, shaking his head. "You don't always have to do what Hewson says." He glanced at her one more time before turning around and walking away.

Hewson's anger flared to her. "I thought you said everything between you was over."

"It is."

"Then what the heck was that?" Hewson yelled.

She looked around at Aycee and the others standing by the fire. "Would you be quiet? Everyone's looking at us."

"I don't care who hears me. I don't care if Beck hears me. In fact, I hope he hears me!" he yelled even louder over his shoulder. "Stay away from my sister!"

Novah grabbed Hewson's arm, pulling him away from all the watchful eyes. She was glad he came without a fight. She didn't think her ankle would stand a chance against him.

"I want you to stay away from him." Hewson pointed an accusatory finger at her.

"Stop freaking out. It was just a hug. You're acting like Beck is some kind of murderer or something."

"He might as well be. That's how much I can't stand

the guy. He's constantly undermining me in the meetings, voting the opposite way, shooting my ideas down."

"I think you're being dramatic."

Hewson's eyes narrowed in on her. "Why are you defending him?"

"I'm not. I'm just saying you need to get over this obsession with Beck."

"Oh, so now it's an obsession?"

"Sometimes it feels like it."

Hewson shook his head, breathless from anger. "Probably because you don't listen. I've lost track of how many times I've asked you to stay away from him."

"What are you even talking about? I gave him up...*for you*. I told him last year that things were over, and I sent him away. What more do you want from me?"

Tears gathered in her eyes as she turned to walk away.

She had nothing left to give.

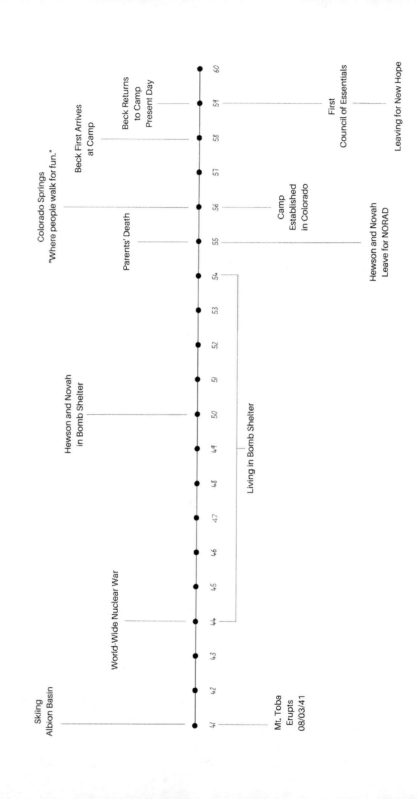

Skiing
Albion Basin

Colorado Springs
"Where people walk for fun."

Beck First Arrives
at Camp

Beck Returns
to Camp
Present Day

World-Wide Nuclear War

Hewson and Novah
in Bomb Shelter

Parents' Death

First
Council of Essentials

41 42 43 44 45 46 47 48 49 50 51 52 53 54 55 56 57 58 59 60

Mt. Toba
Erupts
08/03/41

Living in Bomb Shelter

Camp
Established
in Colorado

Hewson and Novah
Leave for NORAD

Leaving for New Hope

21

Beck

Beginning of Summer 2058 - A Little Over a Year Ago

"I wish I had a s'more to roast for you," Beck said, hugging Novah closer to him.

They sat next to a small fire that Beck had made down where the animals were kept. It was well past midnight, and everyone was asleep. But Novah insisted they waited until the middle of the night to spend time with each other so that Hewson wouldn't find out.

Beck was tired of the sneaking around, but he'd take time with Novah any way he could get it. Especially like this. He imagined this was what a date felt like. Something that a pre-Desolation couple would've done— minus the lack of food and s'mores.

Novah sighed, pressing her back against his chest. "I can't even remember what s'mores taste like. I was so young when we moved to the bomb shelter."

"To tell you the truth, I can't remember either."

She lifted her head, throwing him a playful smile. "Beck Haslett, tell me something else about you I don't know."

Something she didn't know?

Beck was dying to tell her—*for real*—that he loved her. A few weeks ago, he'd poured his heart out in a proposal that didn't go well. But could he really blame Novah? It was his fault for straddling the line between pretend and real.

Instead of confessing his love, he decided to keep things simple.

"Have I ever told you about my first time seeing snow? Or at least I thought it was snow."

"I don't think so." Novah shook her head against his chest.

"I was nine years old, living in North Carolina, and had never seen snow before. I went outside to play, but the sky was dark, like the clouds were folding in on us. I looked down, and it was as if someone had poured powdered sugar all over our lawn. I called for my mom and sisters, yelling for them to come outside. It was snowing in the middle of August. It wasn't even cold outside."

"But it wasn't snow?"

"Nope. It was volcanic ash, blotting out the sun, sailing through the sky, landing on cars and streets."

"I was too young to remember the volcanic winter,

but Hewson has a similar story to yours. You guys have more in common than you think."

They had one thing in common: they both wanted Novah to be happy. But they had very different ideas about what would get her to that point.

He shrugged. "I don't hate him."

"I know." She was thoughtful for a moment. "I can't say he feels the same."

"Yes, his hatred for me runs deep." He hesitated, not sure if he should really say what's been on his mind. "I just hate how he treats you. I don't understand why you let him control you so much."

"He doesn't control me. He's just trying to protect me."

"More like walk all over you."

Her body tensed. "That isn't true."

"Yes, it is." Beck inclined his head toward her. "I know you, Novah. You have a mind of your own. You wouldn't just let someone walk all over you for no reason. Why do you let him get away with it?"

"Hewson is family, and nobody has family anymore. In all three camps, there's only a handful of people who are blood-related, and Hewson and I are two of them." Her shoulders lifted. "I can't ignore something like that."

"That doesn't excuse how he treats you and manipulates you into thinking that you have to obey him."

"He has good reason for it."

A humorless laugh billowed out of him. "Are you seriously saying he has a good reason for being a jerk?"

"I don't expect you to understand."

"Good. Because I don't."

"I'm not an idiot. I know how it looks and how Hewson comes across." She exhaled. "I don't love how he talks to me or the way he bosses me around. I'm not some passive woman who doesn't have the nerve to stand up to her brother."

"Then, why don't you say something to him?"

"Trust me, I have plenty of thoughts in my head, and sometimes I want to unleash them. Like how he thinks I'm worthless and can't contribute because of my foot."

Beck gritted his teeth just thinking about all the times he'd heard Hewson talk down to her because of her injury. "Don't even get me started on this topic. The only reason why I haven't punched him in the face is out of respect for you. I don't want to make your life harder."

She spun around in his arms so she faced him. "You don't make my life harder. If anything, you make me not want to care about what Hewson thinks because *you* make me feel strong and normal—like I can do the same things as everyone else. So, it doesn't matter what Hewson says."

Beck loved that he could give her that confidence. When they'd first met, he wanted nothing more than to help her see her potential, help her find happiness in the journey. To hear that he'd actually reached his goal was the best compliment in the world.

He lifted his lips into a mischievous smile. "So, you're saying you don't want me to punch your brother?"

"He probably deserves it sometimes." She tilted her mouth toward his, softly kissing him.

Beck reciprocated by pulling her body down on top of his. He cupped her cheek with his hand as his lips conveyed all of his feelings of love. Their mouths moved in rhythm together, feeding the flame hotter and hotter. One hand slid under her hair, holding the base of her neck tenderly, keeping her with him as if she might suddenly disappear like everyone else he'd cared for in his life. The other hand inched up her shirt until his fingers felt the ridges on her back. He loved the softness of her body, the familiarity of her hands on him, the understanding of how their lips played with each other's.

There was nothing about her that Beck didn't know.

The kiss unveiled her soul—the heartache, the fear, the strength, the fragility, the broken past, and the hope of a better future.

She loved him.

Beck knew it.

Even if Novah was afraid to say it out loud.

Beck knew it from the way she kissed him.

He rolled her over so his body was on top of hers. They broke apart just for a second. There was a longing in her eyes that matched his, and he knew this moment was special. She nodded, giving her approval. Willpower was normally Beck's strength, but not when it came to Novah. He wanted her body and her soul, and she wanted that, too.

He dipped his head down, kissing her cheek and neck

as his lips traveled lower to her collarbone. But strong hands clamped down on his shoulders, tearing him away from her. Beck sat back in the dirt just in time to see Hewson lunge his body forward. His lowered shoulder hit Beck's stomach, and his arms wrapped around his waist, knocking Beck to his back. Hewson threw a jab to Beck's side as they wrestled.

At first, no one seemed to be winning—their determination equally matched.

Hewson's elbow slammed into the side of Beck's head. A drop of blood trickled down the side of his cheek, but even with the blow, Beck gained the advantage. He twisted their bodies so he was on top and pinned Hewson's back against the ground.

"Beck, stop!" Novah screamed behind him. "Don't hit him!"

Don't hit him?

He hit me!

He tackled me!

"See, Novah?" Hewson hissed between heavy breaths. "Beck is nothing but trouble."

Trouble? Beck loved this woman and would do anything for her. Why couldn't her brother see that?

He grabbed Hewson by the collar of his shirt, pulling him up and slamming him into the dirt again. "I love her and treat her how she deserves to be treated. That's more than I can say for you."

"I know your game. You're trying to turn her against me." Hewson laughed, mocking him. "But it won't work." Hewson shifted his head toward his sister. "Novah's loyalties lie with me."

Beck turned his head, looking into her brown eyes. He waited for her answer, hoped that she'd prove Hewson wrong, that she'd use some of that backbone she'd talked about earlier to finally stand up to her brother. Because deep down, Beck knew the truth. She loved him. She had to. She couldn't fake the feelings that had developed between them over the last few months.

The firelight glistened in her eyes, revealing fresh tears. But she didn't say anything.

"Get off me." Hewson pushed Beck's chest, coming to his feet.

Beck stood, too, waiting for her move.

Instead, her eyes dropped. "Just go, Beck."

Disappointment flowed through his body. He'd wanted Novah to be loyal to *him*, not Hewson. But she couldn't do it.

"Fine." He took a step back, wiping at the blood on his head. Then, he turned around and left.

Novah

"HOW COULD YOU DO THIS TO ME?" Hewson spat. Dirt was smeared across his face, and his lip was cut from the scuffle.

"I'm not doing anything *to* you," she defended.

"You knew how I felt about him. You knew that I didn't want him anywhere near you. I made that very clear. And then, what do you do? You lie to me. You sneak around behind my back with that *snake*."

"I don't understand why you hate him so much. He makes me happy."

"Oh, yeah!" He huffed. "I overheard all about that. How he makes you feel strong and how I treat you like you're worthless."

Her mouth dropped. "You were spying on me?"

"I had to. You left me no choice." He shook his head, lowering his voice. "Don't you see, Novah? Beck's trying to turn you against me. He's putting thoughts in your head that I'm a jerk and that I don't take care of you. I could've left you to die in Kansas, but I didn't. I carried you hundreds of miles to safety."

"I know." Her shoulders dropped. "And I'm grateful, but—"

"If that's true... If you're so grateful for everything I've done for you, then draw the line."

She blinked back at him. "Draw what line?"

"The line between me and Beck. Enough is enough. It's time for you to choose sides. It's either me or him."

"No!" Her head kicked back. "I'm not choosing between you two."

"Why not?"

"Because you're asking too much."

"I'm asking too much," he scoffed.

"Yes. I've already done so much. You asked me to walk across Kansas and Colorado and come to this stupid place. I did that, didn't I?" Tears pricked at her eyes.

"And I was right! I'm always right, Novah!" His voice was picking up strength again. "Why can't you just learn to listen to me? If you listen to me, nobody gets hurt."

Hewson wasn't just talking about Beck. The meaning in his words was written behind his eyes. They had never talked about the day their parents had died. Had never talked about how it was all Novah's fault and how Hewson had told her not to leave the garage. But she didn't listen. She didn't listen, and her parents died.

The details of that awful day were always fresh in her mind, thanks to her recurring nightmares.

The moisture that had gathered around her eyes brimmed over, spilling down her cheeks without restraint as she waded through her brother's words. She couldn't believe that, after all these years, Hewson was finally holding that moment over her head. Could she blame him?

"This infatuation you have for Beck isn't real. It's just the crying baby, and Beck is just another kind of tornado ripping through our family. If he tears us apart, he kills the only thing that's left of our family. Do you really think Mom and Dad would want that?"

Hewson wasn't holding back any punches. He'd gone for the knockout, and Novah felt it everywhere in her chest.

"Just listen to me this one time," he begged. "Don't

you think you owe me for everything that's happened? Don't you think you owe me just this one time?"

She did owe him.

This was his Get Out of Jail Free card, and he was cashing it in.

"Stay away from Beck, okay?"

"Okay," she conceded. "I can do that for you."

The line had been drawn, and Novah had picked her side.

Maybe now, her debt to her brother would finally be repaid.

22

Novah

Spring 2055 - Four Years Ago

Heavy rain poured, and loud wind whirled around Novah's family. It didn't take a meteorologist to know the storm was gaining traction.

Novah curled into herself even more and tightened her arms over her head as if that could save her from the howls. The tornado-like weather had taken her family by surprise as they trekked across Kansas. Her father had led them to a parking garage to take cover. It didn't have a basement level, but it was the best they could find for protection.

She huddled together with Hewson against one wall while her parents hid behind a metal door.

"I think the eye of the storm is coming," her father yelled over to them. "It will all be over soon."

A baby's cries carried with the wind swirling through

the garage.

Novah lifted her head. "Do you hear that?"

"What?" Hewson asked.

"The crying. Do you hear it?"

Hewson pointed to his ear. "The storm's so loud. I can't hear anything."

She held her breath, straining to listen. The wails got louder, and her eyes widened to Hewson. "It's a baby. There's a baby out there." Her already thrumming heart drummed harder.

"So?"

"So we have to do something." She moved to stand, but Hewson caught her hand.

"Are you crazy?"

"We have to save it from the storm."

He gripped her wrist. "You can't go out there. It's not safe."

"What about the baby?" The crying roared in the distance.

"That baby is as good as dead. Leave it alone."

"I can't."

"I'm warning you, Novah. Sit back down, or else you'll put us all in danger."

Novah looked at her brother's stern expression and yanked her hand out of his grasp. She took off running toward the crying before Hewson could stop her. She didn't worry about her safety. All she could think about was finding the crying baby.

"Novah, no!" her mother called, but it was too late.

She was already making her way out of the parking garage.

She fought against the pelting wind and rain, checking cars and looking under things. She had to find the baby before the storm got to it first.

"Novah, come back!" Her mother stood at the edge of the garage, gesturing for her to return to safety. Her dad was there, too, holding onto her mom's shoulders, keeping her from running after Novah.

They beckoned to her, but she couldn't stop. She had to find the baby and take it back with her to where it was safe.

The rain and the wind died down, and the sky above her turned green and eerie. The storm stopping made it easier to hear the cries. She rushed to a storefront. The glass window was shattered, and the siding was gone from the front. Half the roof was missing, and so was the door.

She lifted a pile of debris that had fallen from the store's exterior, and her heart sank.

It wasn't a baby.

It was a Take Care of Me Trudy Doll—the one that came out right before Desolation. It had a computer chip inside of it that mimicked real baby cries. A piece of the metal awning from the storefront had fallen and pushed on the doll's stomach, making it cry.

As soon as Novah realized her mistake, she turned to go back, but the ground rumbled as if a herd of elephants or a train was coming right at her. The sound terrified her, like the devil was coming. In the distance, the tornado's funnel cloud tore up the ground, circling its way closer to them. She crawled to the store entrance, using the outer wall to shield her from danger. Debris flipped and tossed through the air, sending objects flying in every direction. Just as she went to tuck her legs to her chest, a cinderblock from above landed on her right foot, crushing her ankle. She screamed in agony as pain shot through her body. Her teeth gritted together as she pushed the cinderblock off, but the damage was already done. Her foot was limp and mangled. There was no way she could make it back to the garage before the spinning storm reached her. Everything seemed so hopeless.

This was the end.

All the years of hiding out in a bomb shelter were for nothing.

Novah was going to die.

Tears poured from her eyes as she looked back at her parents for help. Her mother must've felt the gravity of the moment, because she cried out in desperation, flipping her head from the funnel cloud back to where she lay by the store.

She wiggled out of her father's grasp and ran toward Novah as if she could somehow save her.

"Madison, no!" Her father followed.

Behind them, the tunnel cloud spun like the Tasmanian Devil.

"Stop!" she cried to her parents. "Go back!"

But it was too late.

The wind was deadly, and her parents were in its direct path. The funnel tumbled down the road, picking up whatever it could and spinning it into the air. A parked car on the street got sucked in. It almost looked like a toy Matchbox car the way it was rotating and flying toward her parents.

"No!" She reached out just as the car slammed into her parents. They didn't even see it coming. It slammed their helpless bodies into the tube of dust and debris—their screams muffled by the swirling wind.

They were gone, and there was nothing Novah could do about it.

All because of her and that stupid Take Care of Me Trudy Doll.

She should've stayed put. She should've listened to Hewson.

The wind followed the funnel, dying down around her.

She sat on the sidewalk, letting her sobs wrack her body.

Hewson peeked his head out of the garage. "What happened? Where's Mom and Dad?"

She couldn't answer.

She didn't need to answer.

His eyes followed where the funnel touched down in the distance, and he knew.

Novah would never forget the look of agony in his eyes. She was the one that put it there.

It was her fault.

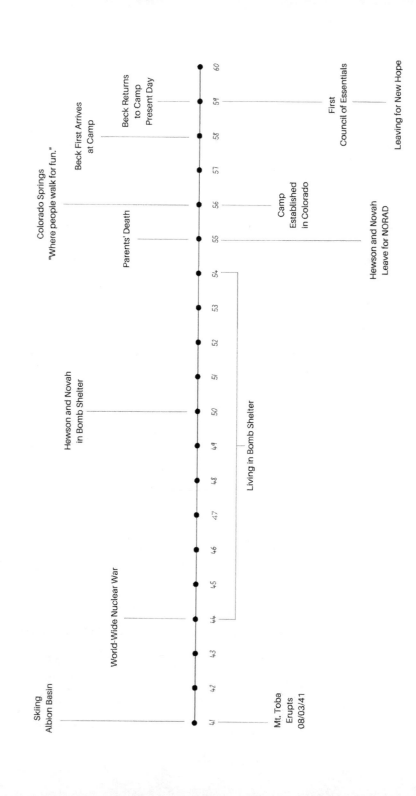

Skiing
Albion Basin

Mt. Toba
Erupts
08/03/41

World-Wide Nuclear War

Hewson and Novah
in Bomb Shelter

Living in Bomb Shelter

Parents' Death

Colorado Springs
"Where people walk for fun."

Camp
Established
in Colorado

Hewson and Novah
Leave for NORAD

Beck First Arrives
at Camp

Beck Returns
to Camp
Present Day

First
Council of Essentials

Leaving for New Hope

41 42 43 44 45 46 47 48 49 50 51 52 53 54 55 56 57 58 59 60

23

Beck

Summer 2059 - Present Day

I t had been two months since the first Council of Essentials meeting. They'd spent most of their time discussing their basic needs: food, water, shelter, and clothing, and how they would make sure each kingdom had those needs met.

Beck had suggested the council choose leaders among the three camps who were experts in each of those fields to train and teach other survivors. Landon, the botanist who had been in charge of the crops at camp, wouldn't be able to go to all seven kingdoms. He needed to share his knowledge so that each kingdom could farm success-fully without him. That was how it was with each essential item.

Driggs, an engineer from Boston, was leading up the training on water and aqueducts. His team of people included survivors with special knowledge in science. They brainstormed about contamination and conservation.

There were several contractors throughout camp that were training others on how to build shelters and what materials were best to use with their limited resources. They focused on how to recycle debris and partial buildings that had withstood the disasters of the last seventeen years and how to make tools.

The council neared the end of their planning. It was time to stop talking about a rebuild and actually go out and start rebuilding from the ground up.

Beck liked the excitement that was in the air. Survivors weren't just surviving anymore. They were using their knowledge, learning new skills, and brainstorming solutions—all under the direction of the seven members of the Council of Essentials.

Beck was the last member of the council to arrive at the meeting that morning. He pulled out his chair and sat down, using his body to scoot the chair forward.

"We're ready to start the meeting," Alexis said with her usual political smile. "I think the training on each essential item is going well. All of us should be able to take the knowledge into our own kingdoms and implement it." She let out a small laugh. "It's actually been kind of fun learning how things were done in ancient times, experimenting with methods from a much simpler era. Of course, we have thousands of years of knowledge on our side to help us, but the methods being used are primitive, and I like that."

"I appreciate that we're returning to a much simpler way of life," Grenham said. "That kind of lifestyle lasted for thousands of years. Much longer than our computer-driven, technological world did. And look what good that did all of us."

"Yes," Alexis agreed. "Before I write up the final Essentials treaty for all of us to sign tomorrow, I want to make sure I understand correctly everything we've decided the last two months."

Tomorrow.

That meant that today was the last meeting.

The finality of it all made Beck anxious. Had the council thought through everything? Had they made the right decisions? Were the survivors really ready to leave camp and travel into the unknown? If it came to it, was Beck ready to leave Novah for good?

He didn't want to choose between leading New Hope to something great or staying with Novah. Even if he stayed, he didn't know how many years it would take for her to let her guard down completely or *if* she ever would.

That was a big risk to take.

Alexis went over the list of basic laws that they'd established, but when she got to weapons, the tension around the table thickened.

"I know we've already talked about guns and weapons, but I urge you all to reconsider." Marcus looked around the table. "I hate that we're stipulating how people can protect themselves. It's a basic freedom to be able to protect yourself and your family. If that means we all have guns, then so be it."

"We can't think like that anymore." Beck turned to him. "I know gun control was a big deal before Mt. Toba erupted, but everything is different now. There are no guns anymore, and we don't have the resources to make guns a priority. We're not trying to take away people's freedoms or say that they can't protect themselves. We're just trying to make sure resources aren't overused or abused. Guns can't be essential right now."

"Do you all agree? Do we need to open this back up for discussion?" Alexis asked, sweeping her eyes around the table.

Andres leaned forward. "If we don't include guns, how are we supposed to kill animals to eat?"

"We shouldn't be killing animals to eat," Beck said logically. "There's not enough of them. If we kill what's left, then they'll go extinct."

Danny looked at Alexis. "We don't need to reopen past discussions, or we'll never be done here. We already voted that guns weren't essential. It's time to move on."

Marcus leaned back into his chair, raising his hands in defeat. "Fine. No guns. No weapons."

He'd agreed to let the subject drop, but there was a defiance in his eyes that gave Beck the feeling this wouldn't be the end of that conversation.

"Various types of weapons are not essential. Not just guns," Hewson added. "A knife is all we need."

"Hewson is right." Andres nodded. "Don't forget to add to the treaty that weapons of mass destruction aren't deemed essential."

"Don't worry. I've already got that part written out. I don't think we want our posterity to live through another nuclear war."

"As time passes, what if we need to make changes to the treaty?" Beck asked. "What if we, as a people, become more sophisticated and are ready for more? As you grow as a people, the more you are ready for additional things to be essential."

"We could meet as a council every ten years and evaluate what is essential?" Marcus clasped his hands together, letting them rest on the table. "We could each come back here in ten years with ideas from our kingdom on what we'd like to see become essential. Then, as a council, we can vote on new items and add them to the treaty. That way, every kingdom is progressing at the same rate. No kingdom becomes more powerful than another. I think that would help keep kingdoms safe from each other and from war."

Hewson perked up. "Ten years is perfect. If a leader is doing well, they could potentially be involved in two to three Council of Essentials during their reign. That kind of longevity would really be beneficial when meeting together."

Beck had to force his eyes not to roll. Hewson didn't

really care about the benefits of longevity. He was only interested in keeping the power for himself. He had to be involved in every decision.

"The only thing I think we should add is a rotation," Danny said. "A different kingdom should host the council every ten years so that we can all see how other kingdoms are progressing."

"Fabulous idea, Danny. A Council of Essentials will be held every ten years to vote on new essential items." Alexis grinned with excitement. "You guys, this system is new and well thought out. I'm so excited. I feel like we should high-five or something."

"How about we all just sign the final treaty and uphold the plan we've set forth?" Marcus said dryly.

Alexis gave a dramatic nod. "Yes, we should all do that, too."

Beck glanced down.

He *was* excited about this new world they'd created, but in the back of his heart, he couldn't get rid of the gnawing feeling that his time with Novah was running out.

He didn't want to go to New Hope without her.

But what happened if he couldn't convince her?

What would happen if she rejected him again?

24

Beck

Beginning of Summer 2058 - A Little Over a Year Ago

After the fight with Hewson, when he'd caught them together, thoughts of Novah played through Beck's mind when he should've been sleeping. All the things he wanted to say to her rolled like a spinning wheel, round and round, in his mind.

It was almost morning. Beck crept off his blanket at the back of the cave, slowly worming his way through the sleeping bodies until he got to Novah. He stopped for a second, soaking in her sleeping beauty.

Then, she moved. She was awake. She rolled over, sensing him. She leaned up on her elbows, letting her eyes adjust. Beck put one finger to his lips, signaling her to be quiet, while the other hand reached out for her. Silently, she moved off her mattress and put on her shoes.

Beck's outreached hand stayed steady, waiting for her to grab it and follow him.

Their steps were slow out of the cave, discreet. Beck took a purple-flowered blanket hanging over the back of a couch and silently slung it around Novah's shoulders. Even though it was summer, there was a chill in the early morning air. They didn't talk as Beck led her, hand in hand, away from camp, up the hill, into the trees.

They stopped, hidden behind thick pines. Beck turned to look at her. He could see the features of her face through the diffused morning light. He pulled her into a tight hug, letting his chin rest on her head. Her face nuzzled into his neck, searching for warmth and comfort.

They stood together as time stretched on, their arms locked tightly around each other.

"I'm sorry about last night with Hewson," he finally said. "If I could do it all over again, I would."

"I know. Me, too." She buried her head deeper into him. Her tears hit his skin, wetting his neck and collarbone.

"Hey!" He pulled back, looking at her. "Don't cry. Things aren't that bad." His mouth tilted into a small smile. "Eventually, Hewson will get over hating me. And when he does, there won't be anything stopping us from being together. You'll see."

"No." She shook her head, pushing away from his body. She wiped at her cheeks and lifted her chin, a resoluteness set on her brow. "It's over."

"What's over?"

"You and me."

Beck's brows dropped. "Wait. What?"

"I'm ending things between us."

He felt the panic of the moment everywhere—in his heart, his mind, his lungs.

"Why? Because of Hewson?"

"Not just because of him. But yes, he's a big part of it."

"When you picture your future in twenty years, are you still following Hewson around? Is being Hewson's sister the only thing you want out of your life?"

"No."

"Then you need to see what it's like living without Hewson. Maybe move to a different camp. I don't know, just anything to gain some space from him."

Novah brushed her hand across her forehead, letting out a heavy breath. "He's my family." Her voice matched her expression, tired and out of fight.

"I know that, but I could be your family, too."

"It's not the same."

"You're right. It's not the same. He's your brother. He can't make you laugh, or hold you, or kiss you the way I can." Beck stepped forward, gently taking her hands in his. He took a chance. He said the vulnerable words he had been keeping in for months. "I love you, Novah. And I think you love me, too."

She bit her top lip and shook her head. "What we

had was so much fun. Some of the best times of my life. But it's over now."

"It doesn't have to be over." He tried pulling her into a hug, but she took a step back.

"Yes, it does."

It was like losing his mom and sisters all over again. He felt helpless, unable to stop the outside forces that kept him from what he wanted.

"You're choosing Hewson over me? Over your own happiness?"

She shifted her weight. Beck saw the agony of the moment written across her face as well. "I don't expect you to understand."

"I don't understand." Emotion laced his words. "I don't understand how you let him manipulate you into this decision."

"What you call manipulation, I call paying him back."

Beck's brows furrowed. "You're not in his debt, Novah."

"Yes, I am." Tears hung precariously on the brims of her eyes, and she dropped her shoulders in defeat. "I'm sorry, but it's over."

Each of her footsteps backward crushed a piece of his heart. The palm of his hand slowly moved to his chest as he watched the love of his life walk away from him.

25

Novah

Summer 2059 - Present Day

The round table from the Council of Essential meetings had been moved down from the tree where the seven leaders had been meeting and situated out in the open by the animal pasture. Thousands of survivors funneled through the line all morning to see the signed Essentials Treaty laid out on the table. There were actually seven copies of the treaty. Alexis had hand-written one for each of the kingdoms to have. The seven leaders signed each one, but only one copy was displayed.

Novah walked slowly through the line. It was her turn to look at all that the council had accomplished in the last two months. But when she looked at Beck's signature on the document, she didn't see the future. She saw despair.

She'd pushed him away so far that she'd forced him

to leave her for good and go to New Hope. The pain of losing him suffocated her. It smothered out all her happiness and hope. All that would be left was a shell of a person, going through the motions of her treacherous life. This kind of hurt was the exact reason she'd convinced herself that they couldn't be together.

Hewson wasn't the *only* thing holding Novah back. But she used his disapproval as a shield to cover up the real reason—the fear of loving Beck wholly and then losing him. She couldn't survive another loss like that. She thought it was easier to protect her heart than shatter it.

But Beck would never understand that reasoning.

He was Mr. Brightside.

Mr. Choose Happiness Over Fear.

He would try to talk her out of her feelings and tell her just to trust or have faith. But Novah wasn't built the same way as him, and she wasn't sure that her love for Beck was enough to rewire her brain. Inevitably, she'd always end up at this crossroad—the pivotal place where she took a leap of faith and chose Beck, or where she succumbed to her greatest fears.

But either way, it seemed like she couldn't win. If he left her for New Hope, she'd be broken. If she went with him, she'd lose him to the elements and be broken.

Maybe her heart was always meant to be shattered.

After a few hours, the line of people died down. The treaty was rolled up and tucked away. The round table was carried back to camp. Everything was done. The

Council of Essentials was officially over for the next ten years.

How would it be when Beck came back ten years from now? Would he be in love with someone else? Ten years wasn't enough time to get him out of her heart. She'd live with this love alone and pray that something would kill her, too.

Novah sat on the brown couch—that most likely started white—and stared blankly into the orange and red dancing flames in front of her. Her legs were crossed. The tip of her foot shook nervously back and forth, but she didn't even notice. Her elbow rested on the arm of the couch, her wrist propping up the side of her face.

"You seem depressed," Hewson said, sitting beside her on the couch.

"I'm fine," she sputtered back. She glanced away, hoping he'd take the hint and leave her alone.

"I just thought you'd be happier with the rebuild figured out. Our future is about to get exciting."

"I said I was fine." She snapped her head back in his direction.

Hewson hesitated to respond, clearly not sure how to handle his sister's moodiness. "Is this about Beck?"

Novah glared at her brother, unwilling to give him an answer.

"I knew this would happen." He huffed. "I told you that guy was trying to tear us apart. He's gotten in your head and ruined everything."

Beck was definitely in Novah's head, but not in the

way Hewson thought. Her heart was filled with him. Every happy moment they shared found a way to torment her thoughts. He was her only chance for a happy future, but now the future was about to pass her by.

People had made their choices of which of the seven kingdoms they were going to live in. Some people chose based on where they wanted to live. Some people made their decision because they wanted to follow a certain leader. Either way, people were choosing their future. Not Novah, though. She was held captive by her fear, letting the world and life happen around her.

Fear was a part of her just as much as breathing was.

Perhaps it was something she'd learned from her parents from hiding out in a bomb shelter her entire childhood and teenage years, only being allowed outside for short periods of time. Scared of everything. When the food ran out and they were forced to leave the shelter, her parents died.

Now, the fear of living without Beck weighed her down.

"I'll be glad when he's out of our life for good." Hewson puffed out his chest. "Trust me, you're better off without him."

"What if I'm not?" Her words came out like daggers aimed at her brother. "What if you're wrong about him?"

"I'm never wrong." He stood, looking down at her.

"Just don't do something stupid like thinking you're going to go with him. Don't hurt me like that." Emotion filled his eyes. Novah had only seen her brother cry one other time.

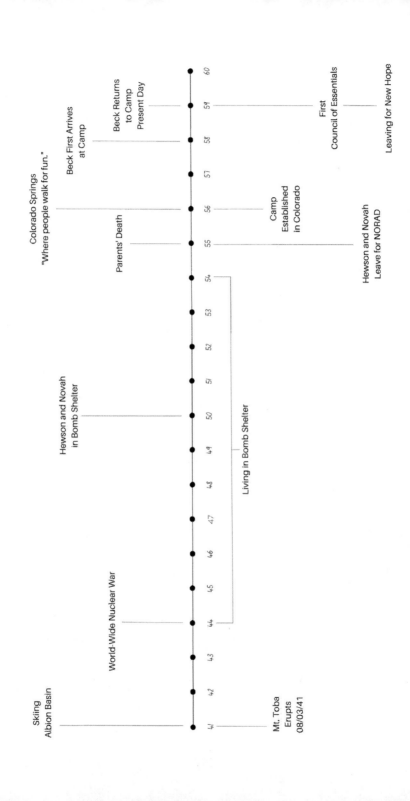

26

Novah

Spring 2056 - Three Years Ago

"Look how close we are to the mountain." Hewson excitedly climbed over rows and rows of cracked wreckage, leaving Novah to fend for herself behind him. When she was too slow, he reached down and grabbed her hand, helping pull her up. "Watch your step." He pointed to a piece of sharp rebar sticking out of concrete. "I think the opening to NORAD will be just beyond this mound."

Novah wasn't so sure. Everything was so torn up from the last earthquake. It was like the entire landscape of the area had been changed. There was no way the NORAD base was unscathed.

"We might not find anything." Her words came out choppy as all her energy went to ignoring the ache in her ankle.

"Yes, we will." There was an unmistakable determination in Hewson's voice.

"But the government stopped calling people to NORAD. We don't know what's happened out here." She glanced around at the rubble of concrete around them. "By the looks of things, there was a pretty big earthquake or two, and we haven't heard anything on the radio for years."

"If there were earthquakes, I'm sure it just cut off their communication. The base was built to withstand everything."

She hoped he was right. She hoped that climbing over broken trees, mounds of dirt, and huge boulders bigger than semi-trucks on her bad foot would all be worth it. It took a while to find a passable route, but eventually, they made it.

Hewson saw it first.

"No," he breathed out. "No." He frantically walked back and forth, searching.

Novah stared blankly ahead at the mountain of rocks and ginormous boulders piled in front of them. A few pieces of the torn-up road led to the pyramid of rocks before them. Some pieces were even painted with yellow lines that used to divide the highway.

There was nowhere else to go.

No way into NORAD.

A blockade of impenetrable rocks and boulders covered what was once the entrance.

A dead end.

Hewson uttered a gut-wrenching scream as he kicked at the debris around him. Novah covered her mouth with her hands as she watched her brother lose his mind. He grabbed anything he could lift, throwing it wildly in front of him. Her own tears fell steadily as Hewson's angry screams filled the air, echoing off the mountain into the valley below. There was nothing she could do but watch. His mental toughness had been broken.

"All of this was for NOTHING!" he yelled, falling to his knees. His hands flew to his face, and a sob croaked out of his throat. She rushed to his side, hugging him tight against her chest.

"It'll be alright," she whispered as she pushed his hair away from his forehead. "It'll be alright."

Hewson sobbed for hours in her arms, letting out all his pent-up fears and anxieties from the last twelve years. He was like a small child in her arms. Silently, her own tears fell, spilling down her neck and darkening the collar of her shirt. She wanted to crumble to pieces, too, but she knew for once she had to be strong for her brother.

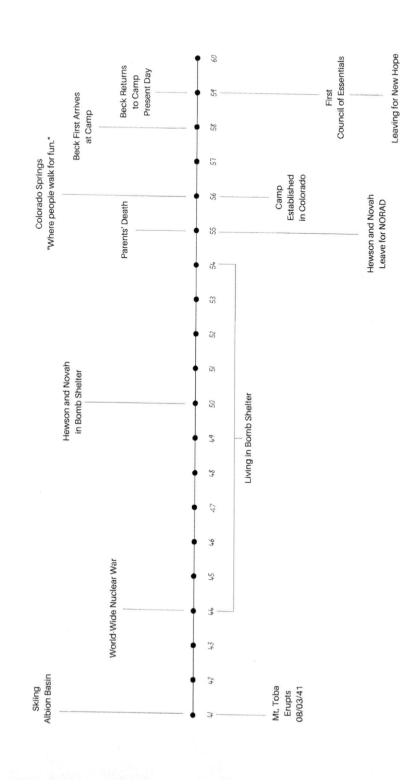

Skiing
Albion Basin

Colorado Springs
"Where people walk for fun."

Beck First Arrives
at Camp

Beck Returns
to Camp
Present Day

Hewson and Novah
in Bomb Shelter

Parents' Death

World-Wide Nuclear War

First
Council of Essentials

Leaving for New Hope

Camp
Established
in Colorado

Hewson and Novah
Leave for NORAD

Living in Bomb Shelter

Mt. Toba
Erupts
08/03/41

41 42 43 44 45 46 47 48 49 50 51 52 53 54 55 56 57 58 59 60

27

Hewson

Summer 2059 - Present Day

Hewson worked side by side with Andres, filling jugs and containers with water for the two parties that were leaving for their kingdoms first. Luckily, it had been decided that Beck's party and Andres's group leaving for Cristole would be the first to leave. Leaving midsummer hopefully put them far enough away that they'd be in warmer temperatures before the harsh winter set in. But none of them knew for sure what the weather would be like. Post-desolation weather had been atypical for years. But they had to stagger out the groups leaving so that they could grow more crops and get more food to supply each caravan. The groups going to Appa, Northland, and Tolsten would leave next spring when the thaw started.

"I don't know what you're so angry about," Andres said. "Beck will be gone in a week and out of your life for good."

"Not for good." Hewson lifted a full jug out of the river and grabbed a new one. "I'll see him in ten years at the next Council of Essentials."

"So? Ten years is so long. Do you know how many things can change before then? He might be dead, and some new leader will come to the Council instead."

"Let's hope he's dead," Hewson muttered.

Andres laughed. "What are you so bitter about?"

Bitter? He was beyond bitter.

"He's turning Novah against me, putting thoughts in her head that she's better off with him instead of me."

"So? Once he's gone and time has passed, things will go back to normal." Andres grunted as he lifted a heavy bucket from the water to the bank.

"No." Hewson stopped working, letting his mind run wild. "This won't go back to normal. The damage has been done."

Beck leaving wasn't enough to rid Novah's mind and heart of him. Hewson had already tried that tactic a year ago. It was his idea to send out a search party for survivors, but he let people believe that Danny had come up with it. He hated handing over the praise to Danny, but it had been a necessary step in his plan. He planted a seed in Danny's mind that Beck and Drew would be the best people to leave camp and lead the search. The dominoes fell in a line after that. All Hewson had to do was sit back and watch the consequences of his manipulation. Danny approached Beck and Drew, and by the time they announced the search to all the camps, Beck raised his hand to volunteer.

"The one year Beck was gone hadn't been enough to break the bond between them. I'm not sure ten years will be enough. As long as he's alive, Novah will always pine for him."

"Well, then she'll always resent you for keeping them apart." Andres shrugged. "You need to put the ball in her court, step back, and let her decide if she wants to go to New Hope or not."

"I can't do that." He shook his head. "I promised my dad nine years ago that if anything ever happened to him, I would take care of Novah and protect her no matter what. How can I keep that promise if she lives in New Hope?"

"Maybe she'll choose you over him. She already did once."

Andres was right. Given the freedom to choose, Novah might stay by his side. Hewson would do anything for her, so why wouldn't she do anything for him? If he gave her the choice and she stayed in Albion, then she couldn't resent him. But was he really prepared to let her leave with Beck?

"If I were you, I'd lay it out on the table. See what she says. If you don't, she'll be angry the rest of her life and hold that anger against you."

Maybe he would let her choose. Surely, she'd see

there was no other choice than to stay with him. Then, Beck would be gone, and Hewson would be the good guy in the situation.

28

Novah

Summer 2059 - Present Day

Five days.

That was all Novah had left with Beck before he traveled to New Hope.

When a person gets close to the end, they think about the past—the journey that got them where they are. Novah had spent all morning reflecting on the ups and downs of their relationship. Love was torture and euphoria combined—a thrilling rollercoaster of emotions that made her sick one moment and then full of exhilaration the next.

Right then, she was in the torture moment.

She had to decide, once and for all, what she was going to do.

Novah stood in the middle of the river, washing their clothes. She'd just finished taking a bath, and since she was already wet, it seemed like a good time to do the laundry.

"How many times have I told you not to go to the river alone?"

She glanced up to face her brother. "If you knew how many times I've come here alone and been just fine, you wouldn't be so worried."

"All it takes is one time for something bad to happen." He stepped into the water, making his way to her. "But you just keep doing stupid things that put you in danger. When will you finally learn that you need to listen to me?" His voice wasn't harsh, but it didn't matter. His words bugged her.

The worst part was that he didn't even recognize how condescending he sounded. It was just who he was— written in his DNA as much as his brown hair. Normally, Novah could let his remarks roll off her back, but not today. Not when she was heartbroken and confused about Beck and everything that was at stake.

She pulled her shoulders back. "Like, how I should have listened to you when our parents died?"

"Yeah." He seemed surprised by her boldness. "I wasn't going to bring it up, but that's the perfect example of what I'm talking about. If you had listened to me, they wouldn't have died."

"You weren't going to bring it up?" The hot anger inside her began to bubble to life. "But yet, you always seem to bring it up. You always seem to find a way to hold their deaths over my head."

"That's not true. I never even talk about it."

"No, you don't *talk* about it. You just imply and insinuate, reminding me daily that it was my fault. Why would you do that? Why would you want me to feel bad about it? You're my brother." Emotion started to creep into her voice.

His expression softened. "I only remind you so that you'll learn."

"It was an accident!" she blurted. "Don't you think that I regret it? Don't you think that if I could do it all over again, I would listen to you and stay in the parking garage?" Steady tears streamed down her face. "Don't you think that I'm sorry?"

"Yes, but—"

"But what?" Her voice was loud. "I already torture myself day in and day out with the guilt. What more do you want from me? When will you forgive me?"

"I don't know." He threw his arms out to the side. "I wish I could say that it's all okay, but it's not. I blame you, and I don't know if I ever *can* fully forgive you."

Novah nodded, blinking to release a fresh wave of tears. "Then, I don't think I can stay here with you. How am I ever supposed to get over their deaths when you're constantly holding it over my head with no end in sight?" She shrugged one shoulder. "You've been manipulating me this whole time, using our parents' deaths as a way to control me. And if I keep letting you do that, I'll never get over the guilt. Maybe Beck was right. Maybe I need to try living my life without you and see what it's like."

"Of course you bring this back to Beck." He placed his hands on his hips, shaking his head. "I came here to tell you that I'm letting you choose if you want to go with Beck to New Hope or if you want to stay here with me. Does that sound like someone who's trying to manipulate you?"

"You're *letting* me choose?" she scoffed. "How nice of you." Her words were full of sarcasm.

"Yeah, well I *wanted* you to choose, but it's clear that Beck's been poisoning you with lies, so I'm not sure your decision-making can be trusted."

"Maybe my decision-making can't be trusted"—she paused, exhaling a breath—"but my heart can. And my heart wants Beck."

Novah had tried to bury her feelings for him deep in the rubble and debris of her shattered heart, but somehow, he'd patched the brokenness back together. She loved him for that and for so many other reasons.

"I love him, Hewson, and if I ever want to find some sort of happiness in this life, then I need to go to New Hope with him."

She stared at her brother's defeated expression. His shaggy hair wisped across his forehead and over his eyebrows. It was almost time for another haircut. If she left with Beck, who was going to cut his hair, or wash his clothes, or sleep on the mattress next to him? Who was he going to tell his secrets to and laugh with? She wouldn't see him be a king, or build Albion, or reach his full potential. But she couldn't reach *her* full potential if she stayed with him. She'd outgrown this place and Hewson's protectiveness. That didn't mean leaving her brother wouldn't hurt. Because although their relationship was complicated, it wasn't *all* bad. There had been some good times, too.

But it was time to let go.

Of the past.

Of the demons that held her back.

Beck was her future now.

Hewson stepped back, leaning against the boulder in the middle of the river. "How could you do this to me? How could you trust him more than you trust me?"

Novah wanted him to see things from her side. "This has nothing to do with trusting Beck over you or what lies you think he's told me about you. It's just what's best for me to move on from the past. It's my chance for true happiness." He dropped his head, and both his hands raked through his hair. She hated hurting him in this way. "Besides, you don't need me. You'll be busy rebuilding this place. You're going to do so many wonderful things in Albion, and I'd just be in the way."

His silence clutched her chest, squeezing it tight. She held her breath, waiting for him to react or respond. There was so much that they should talk about—the hurt, misunderstandings, and pain from the last few years—all the things that had led them to this point. Would he hash it all out? Or would he accept defeat and let her go?

A low-pitched rumble vibrated through the water, up her feet, and to her chest. The ground moved below them, causing Novah to take a few steps just to stay upright. But the shaking was too much. She fell back into the water, landing on her backside. She tried to stand up again but couldn't with the way the earth moved below her.

Hewson reached for her, panic in his eyes as he tried to keep his own footing. "It's an earthquake!"

The trees swayed, and rocks tumbled down the mountain. The river sloshed in her face, carrying her slowly forward with the current as the crashing and cracking roared around them.

Hewson let go of the steadiness of the boulder to help her. He stumbled, crawling after her. Rocks and boulders dropped around them, splashing into the water. Her heart raced, and she felt like she was drowning, even though her hands and feet could touch the bottom. She just couldn't stop herself from moving with the river.

The shaking stopped, but the noise didn't. A different kind of rumbling sound increased in volume. The snapping of trees. The grinding of rocks as they crashed into each other.

"It's a landslide!" Hewson yelled, looking behind them and above them.

Novah tried looking, too, but she couldn't see any immediate threat. Wherever the landslide was, it wasn't coming down on top of them.

Hewson climbed to his feet, rushing to her side. He grabbed under her arms, pulling her to her feet. "Are you okay?"

She was scared but okay. "Yeah."

"We've got to get out of here before the aftershocks come." He wrapped his arm around her waist, leading her to the shore, but before they could get to safety, a new danger threatened them.

It sounded like a waterfall.

They both turned their head to the raging water splashing and gushing toward them. There was no time to react. The rapids knocked their feet out from under them, pushing them underwater, pulling them forward.

Novah twisted in the water. Her knee banged against a rock as she passed by, and she yelped underwater. Her lungs fought for strength until she could find the surface. She gasped for air as her head broke through the water. Hewson was in front of her, being carried away, too.

"Flip to your back! Feet forward!" he called.

She tried to copy his pose, using her hands to fight against the raging water.

A pile of rocks was just ahead of her. If she could grab ahold of them, she might be able to stop herself from being pulled downstream with the rapids.

She kicked her good foot out, trying to connect with the closest boulder. The water spun her body, but it was enough for her hands to reach the slick rock. Her fingers clung to any crack or crevice she could find. She pulled her body to safety, fighting against the current with everything she had until her feet could reach and help with the fight. Her entire body worked, and just when she thought her muscles couldn't take any more, she gained the advantage. Her chest pressed against the rocks. She used her hands and feet to brace herself, holding her firm so the current couldn't take her again.

She glanced up. Hewson clung to a tree branch ten feet from her. She didn't know how long he'd be able to hold on or how long the tree branch would last. She just hoped Beck would find them before it was too late.

Because if she knew anything, she knew Beck would come after her.

29

Beck

Summer 2059 - Present Day

An earthquake.

Beck had been through tsunamis, floods, storms, and hurricanes, but never an earthquake. It took a second for his mind to register what was even happening.

He was back in camp, gathering supplies, when the shaking started.

"Get out of the cave!" he shouted. "It's an earthquake!" A dozen people rushed to the exit, crawling because the rolling ground made it too hard to walk. "Is there anyone else?"

"I don't think so," a woman cried, stumbling past him.

Beck tried to run back toward the center of camp,

but each footstep felt unstable, and his body lurched forward and then sideways. It was like he was running across a rickety old bridge, each step swaying him from side to side. Thunder-like booms cracked all around him, churning his chest. Danny and Drew waved people away from the mountain, trying to get them out in the open and to safety.

Beck was frantic. His eyes darted to the campfire, the couches, and where they prepped food, but Novah was nowhere.

"Novah?" he called to Danny.

"Haven't seen her!"

There was only one other place she'd go. She had to be up the trail at the river—the worst possible place to be. Beck shifted his direction, trying to make it to the trees, but the rattling made every move twice as difficult. Loose rocks rolled down the mountainside, crashing around them.

The ground swayed to a stop, but the rattling of rocks, boulders, and pebbles tumbling down the mountain continued on. He just hoped Novah wasn't in the slide's direct path.

"Novah!" He had to find her before the loose earth became even more dangerous. "Novah!"

Without the shaking, he covered more ground faster, but when he made it to the river, his heart dropped. The rushing water plunged forward, spilling over what used to be the bank, taking everything in its path with it.

"Novah!" he yelled as he took off, running down the side of the river. "Novah!"

"Beck!" His heart raced as he moved to the sound of her voice. He saw her up ahead, holding onto some rocks. Hewson was a few feet in front of her, holding onto a branch.

"Beck! We can't hold on much longer!" Novah yelled.

"Don't worry." He tried to reassure her with a small smile. "I'm coming."

"No, you'll get swept away!" Her tears turned to hysterics. "I can't watch you die because of me."

He glanced around for the best path to cross the rapids, but the current was too strong. Novah seemed to be in a better position than Hewson, and as much as he hated doing it, he ran to him first.

"Let me get something to pull you in." Beck looked around for a bigger branch that he could use. There was a huge log that had fallen from a tree trunk in the earthquake, but it was too big to help Hewson.

"No!" Hewson called. "Save Novah first!"

Beck shook his head. "We can save her together."

"Please!" Hewson begged. "Save Novah. She's my responsibility."

For a split second, Beck stared at him. They both understood what would happen if he saved Novah first. Hewson didn't have the strength to keep holding on, but his eyes screamed that he didn't care. It only mattered that Novah made it out of danger alive.

Beck nodded once in mutual understanding, then ran to the large log. He picked up one end, slowly dragging it over to the water. If he could wedge the piece of wood upstream between the rocks where Novah was and another boulder closer to shore, he could brace himself against it and cross the rapids to her.

"What about Hewson?" she called over to him while he worked to maneuver the log.

"He wanted me to save you first."

Novah's eyes flicked to her brother. "Hewson!"

"I'm good!" He grunted.

But he wasn't good.

Maybe if Beck hurried, he could save them both.

He had one chance to get the tree in the right spot or else it would get swept away. He rotated the log so it stood straight up adjacent to the boulders he needed it to land on.

"Look out. I'm going to drop this down by you."

Novah nodded, scooting as far as she could to the edge of the rocks.

Beck said a quick prayer that his plan would work, then let the trunk fall. Water splashed as the tree submerged, but when it came to the surface, it was fixed between the two boulders right where he'd hoped it would land.

He didn't waste any time. He jumped in the water, keeping his hands pressed against the log so the water didn't carry him away. His gaze darted to Hewson. His hand slipped, and his head kept falling under the water.

Hang on just a little longer, Hewson.

"Beck!" Tears of relief spilled down Novah's cheeks.

She stared back at him for a moment, then nodded. "Almost there."

He didn't stop when he reached Novah. Instead, he scooped her into his arms, hugging her to him. The relief that she was safe made him tighten his hold. Her head buried into his shoulder, and her arms wrapped around his neck, clinging to him.

"Hang on. I'll get you across the river safely."

He slowly inched his hands along the log, keeping his chest pressed against it so he wouldn't get sucked too far under. The shore was nine feet away. His eyes swung to Hewson. He was still there. If he just hurried, he could save Hewson, too.

Four feet away.

The same boom started up again, like rocks grinding together. The ground below them started to sway violently, and the water raised to one side and then back to the other.

Aftershocks.

He pushed Novah forward. She kicked her legs, fighting to finish the last few feet until she could reach the ground. The log moved with the quake and shifted enough that it came undone. Beck felt his body moving forward with the water, but he fought and clawed. His feet hit solid ground, and somehow, he managed to get to the side.

"Hewson!" Novah screamed. She tried to run to him, but the unsteadiness brought her to her knees. "No!"

Beck crawled to her side, hugging her close just as Hewson's tree branch came unearthed from the soil, sending him into the rapids.

She hit against his chest, trying to free herself. "We have to go after him!"

"It's too late."

They could try to go after him after the shaking stopped, but Beck knew it would be a lost cause.

Hewson was gone.

"No!" she cried, clinging to Beck's shirt.

"Shh." He pulled her to him, shielding her body in case a branch or something fell on them. "It's okay."

It seemed like the shaking feeding the seismic monster would never stop. Rocks rolled down the side of the mountain, splashing into the water. Tree branches clapped against each other, adding to the horrific noise.

Then, it all stopped.

Beck picked her up, cradling her body in his arms. He carried her back to camp, her sobbing the entire way.

When they came out of the trees, Danny rushed to them. "Is she okay?"

Beck nodded.

Danny looked behind them. "Where's Hewson?"

His jaw clenched, trying to keep from crying. He shook his head, and Danny understood.

"Bring her to the fire. I'll get some blankets." He rushed off.

Beck sat down in front of the fire with Novah in his lap. Sobs wracked her body as she clung to him.

Hewson had saved her life, and in return, he'd lost his own.

In that *one* moment, Hewson Harper was a good brother.

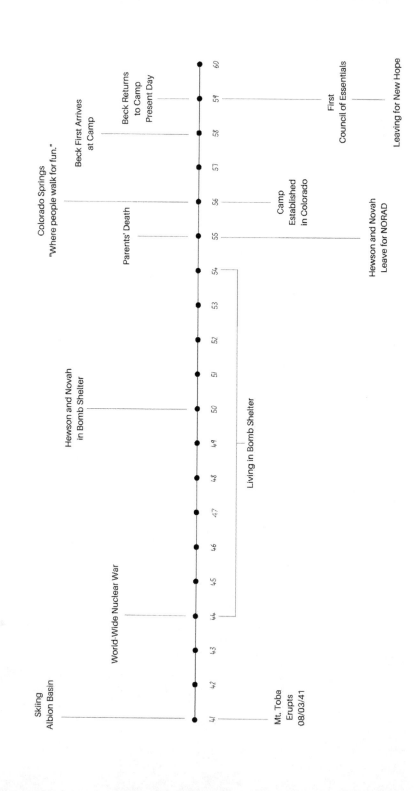

30

Beck

Summer 2059 - Present Day

It had been two hours since the last aftershock. Beck had gotten Novah changed into some dry clothes and had lain her down on a mattress inside the cave. She'd cried herself to sleep in his arms as he gently stroked her hair over and over.

"Beck," she whispered after an hour.

He dipped his chin to see her face. "I thought you were asleep."

Her voice trembled. "Everyone close to me dies because of me."

"Novah"—he turned on his side so his body faced hers—"it's not your fault. It was an earthquake."

He gently caressed her cheek. Written across her expression was her conflicting fear.

Always fear.

Beck would give anything to take that fear away.

"It was my fault my parents died." Her brown eyes were already full of moisture, and her voice was shaky. "We were taking cover from a tornado, and I thought I heard a baby crying, so I went after it. Hewson warned me not to go. He told me it wasn't safe, but I didn't listen. My parents followed after me." Her body quivered against his as she spoke. "But it wasn't even a real baby. It was just a toy, but before I could get back to my parents, a cinderblock fell on my foot." Her eyes dropped. "They ran out into the storm to save me and were swept away."

Beck hugged her and rubbed her back. He'd give anything to take the hurt away from her.

"It was my fault."

Beck had all the pieces to the puzzle now. This was why she let Hewson control her. This was what she'd been holding back this whole time.

"Hey." He pulled back, pushing her chin up with the tips of his fingers. Her gaze was fragile and timid, but she kept it on him. "You can't blame yourself. You didn't make your parents run after you. And what if the baby had been real? You would have saved a life. I think you're brave for risking your life to help."

"Now it's all happening again with Hewson. It's my fault."

"You have to stop blaming yourself for things that are out of your control. It was an innocent accident. You have to let it all go."

Beck hated that she'd been carrying around this guilt

for years. He'd been where she was after his own family had died. He had lived in the past every day, thinking he could somehow fix what had happened, but he'd had to learn the hard way to let the past go.

She looked up at him with her puffy eyes, searching for the truth behind his words. She looked fragile, vulnerable, and painfully beautiful.

Novah

HEWSON WAS GONE.

None of it seemed real.

Novah's natural inclination was to blame herself. If she hadn't been in the river, doing laundry, none of this would've happened. That was where her mind wanted to go.

And to make matters worse, in the last conversation she'd had with Hewson, she'd chosen Beck and broken her brother's heart. That was how things had ended between them.

"This is why you chose Hewson over me." Beck's voice wasn't accusing or even full of hurt. His expression held understanding, as if he was grateful to finally know why.

"It was a big part of it. I felt like I owed Hewson. But more than that…" Her lips trembled as emotion took over. "I'm scared of losing *you*. Everyone that I've ever truly loved has been taken from me. Now Hewson. Logically, you're next. And if I lose you, I won't recover."

"You're not going to lose me." He took her hand in his.

"You can't promise that. Hewson said the same kind of things, and now he's gone."

"Okay, you're right. I can't promise that you won't ever lose me, but isn't it worth the risk?" His lips lifted. "Isn't time together—no matter how long or short—worth the risk of losing your loved ones? You'd never wish that you didn't have all those years with Hewson or with your parents just to shield yourself from the pain of losing them, would you?"

"No."

Novah treasured the time spent with her parents, the years of memories she'd had with them in the bomb shelter, and how their relationship shaped the woman she was today. And since then, the hardships and struggles she and Hewson went through that bonded them together. She'd never trade all of that just to escape the pain of losing them. So why wasn't she willing to face her fears to have that same time with Beck? Because, at the end of the day, wasn't being with him worth every ounce of heartache losing him would cause?

She *wanted* to let go of everything surrounding her parents' death and now Hewson's. She couldn't live with this pain forever. She *wanted* to release herself from the remorse, shame, and guilt, but she didn't know how.

Beck was right. It was time to let the past go, but that didn't mean Novah *could* do it.

She pulled back to look into his hazel eyes. She needed him to see the sincerity behind what she was about to say. "I want to come with you to New Hope. And not because Hewson is gone." Her voice cracked with emotion when she said the words. "Before the earthquake, I told him that I loved you and that I wanted to go with you. I hate that that was our last conversation—me disappointing him—but…"

"Hewson wasn't disappointed in you. *He* told me to save you. He knew the risk and still wanted me to save you. That doesn't sound like a brother that's upset with you over your last conversation. That sounds like a brother who loves you."

A single tear trickled down her cheek and rolled over her lips. After everything that had happened with their parents, and with Beck over the last year and a half, Hewson had sacrificed himself for her. He'd done what he'd promised their dad. He'd protected her no matter what.

"I don't know how to make his sacrifice worthwhile." She bit her lip, trying to keep from crying more. She had a headache from the last two hours of tears.

Beck smiled in his gentle way. "You do it by living your life to the fullest and by being happy."

"I want to be happy, but giving up the past and letting go of my fears are going to take some time. I don't think I can do it alone. I'll need your help."

"I'm here for whatever you need."

"I know. Just be patient with me, okay?"

His smile widened. "I think I've shown I can be patient."

"That's why I love you."

A small laugh puffed over his lips. "You love me?"

Novah's lips pressed into a small smile. "Yes, Beck. I love you."

"I've been waiting a long time for you to say that." His fingers brushed over her cheek.

"I thought that if I didn't say it out loud or even admit it to myself, I could keep my heart safe. But I know now that my heart is the safest *with* you. You're the reason I even believe in love. I thought life was only about hurt and anguish, but then you came along and brightened everything up. You've allowed me to hope again, and I love you for that."

"I love you, too." He smiled. "I've always loved you. Since the moment I met you, I haven't been able to get you out of my heart. It's only ever been you."

"What about Aycee? I'm sure you had a thought about how much easier things would be with her instead of me."

His fingers slid through her hair, tucking it behind her ear. "I think Aycee realized that day I gave you the ibuprofen that she didn't stand a chance. My heart was already yours."

Beck slowly leaned down. It had been over a year since they'd last kissed, but the memory of his lips was burned into her skin. Her heart pounded against her chest as she waited for what she'd been longing for. Their mouths touched, sending a sweet sensation thrumming to her soul. There was a gentleness to his kiss that melted Novah's heart but also a passion that thrilled her. She pulled him closer, kissing him with an intensity that went beyond all their other kisses. She was desperate for him to know, to *feel*, how much she loved him, to make up for all the times she hadn't said it to him when she should've. And for a moment, she thought she'd been spared from Desolation just to know what it felt like to kiss Beck Haslett.

He pulled back, his eyes sweeping across her face. He reached up and brushed her hair back from her face.

"I've missed you."

"I've missed you, too."

She spent the rest of the afternoon in Beck's arms. His presence soothed her loss and healed her soul. And in a way, she wondered if Hewson asking Beck to save her instead of him was his final acceptance that Beck would take care of her.

He'd finally given up control, trusting Beck to protect her.

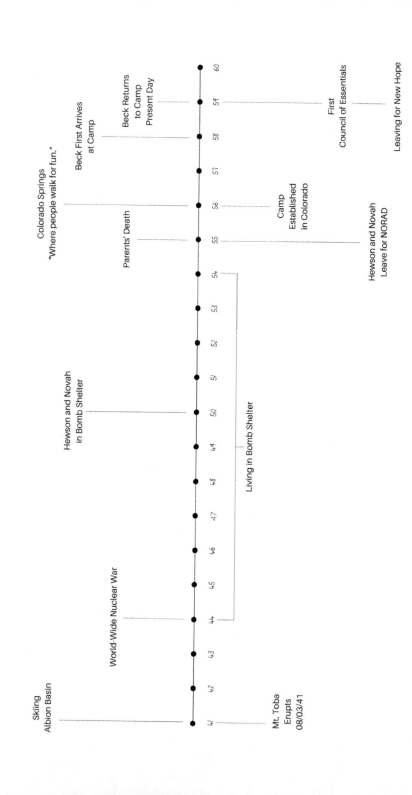

31

Novah

Fall 2059 - Present Day
Two Months Later

B eck threw a blanket on the ground next to a small fire. The caravan had worked for the last hour, clearing debris so they all had a place to sleep that night. They'd been on the road for months, slowly making their way to New Hope. The uneven terrain made things difficult, especially for Novah's ankle. Beck had made her a walking stick from a tree branch that helped for support. They also had to work together to lift the two wagons filled with supplies over all the debris. It was a slow and painful process. Novah had already trekked through what felt like half the United States, but this time, things were different.

This time, she was with Beck.

He smiled at her, gesturing to the make-shift bed. "Ma'am, sleep awaits you."

She frowned as she grabbed his hand and slowly lowered to the ground. "I thought we already talked about you not calling me ma'am."

His eyes glimmered. "Well, I call you a lot of other things in my mind, but they're a little naughty"—he looked around—"and I don't want to embarrass you."

Novah laughed. "Ma'am will work just fine."

He crawled over to her legs and pulled off her shoes, massaging her bad foot.

She lifted onto her elbows. "Beck, you don't have to do this every night. You're sore and tired, too."

"Does it feel good?" He raised his brows.

Her head fell back, and she sighed. "Yes!"

"Then, relax and enjoy it."

"Okay." She fell down to her back again and closed her eyes. "Who do you think won the vote back at camp to be the new leader of Albion?"

"I'm sure Drew won. He's the best choice, and I'm glad he'll get the chance to be a leader."

"What do you think New Hope will be like?" she asked after a minute of silence.

"What? Like, the land?"

"No." She opened her eyes and looked at him. "Like our life."

A smile spread across his face. "Oh, look who's finally excited for the future. What happened to the cynical woman I fell in love with?"

She smirked. "She's still very much here."

"No, I don't think so." He let go of her foot and slowly crawled up her body. Each of his movements was sexy and playful, causing Novah's heart to pound. He leaned on one elbow, hovering over her. "I think you're looking forward to your future with me."

"Well, you are a king," she teased.

"Nah." He brushed her hair back. "I'm just a man in love with you."

Her eyes danced. "Who also happens to be a king."

"A minor detail." He bent down and kissed her cheek. "But if I'm a king, doesn't that make you my queen?" He kissed her other cheek.

"Technically, we're not married, so I'm actually not *your* queen."

"Then, marry me." He kissed her neck.

Her brows raised. "Marry you?"

He paused his kisses and gazed down at her. "Yes, marry me." Sincerity overflowed from his eyes. "I want to build a life with you, starting from the ground up."

"You're already building a life with me."

"But I want it all." He smiled—the one filled with so much joy and optimism. The smile that made Novah fall in love with him when they'd first met. "I want to exchange rings, get married, and have children and grandchildren."

The threat of fear began to creep inside her chest, but she willed it away. Her eyes filled with happy tears. The last few years, she didn't dare picture herself ever getting married or being a mother. She didn't want to hope for something that seemed impossible. He offered her a life—the one Desolation almost took from her.

"And I know this isn't the romantic proposal you or your mother were hoping for. I *literally* have nothing to offer you besides my heart and the promise that I'll always take care of you, but I hope that's enough."

Beck's proposal was more than what her mother had told her about. It was more than magic.

It was real.

"Your heart is all I want." She smiled. "And I'd love to marry you."

Beck laughed like he did the first time they'd kissed. His body fell on top of hers, hugging her tight. He shifted their bodies and brought his mouth to hers. The kiss was full of excitement and happiness, a celebration of how far they'd come.

"Get a room, you two!" Indie joked from the next fire over.

Beck laughed, turning his head to respond back to her. "We would if we could!"

"Isn't this what she wanted?" Novah smirked. "Us to be together?"

"I guess she didn't think about the consequences."

Beck rolled onto his back, pulling her body in close. She rested her head on his chest and felt the strong beat of his heart against her cheek.

"Speaking of getting a room." His tone was wicked.

"I may have saved some lingerie from that store—just in case you came around."

She twisted her head to see him. "I told you I would *never* talk about my underwear with you."

Beck dipped his chin, a playful expression on his face. "Never?"

Her eyes danced up at him. "Never."

"Well, we're going to have to change that."

He kissed her again.

It was just the beginning of their new life beyond Desolation.

Their new hope.

The End

I hope you enjoyed Beck and Novah's story. I love hearing what readers liked most about my books, so don't forget to leave a review and tell me.

Stay connected with me at www.kortneykeisel.com, or follow me on Instagram, Facebook, or Pinterest

Also by Kortney Keisel

The Desolation Series (Dystopian Royal Romance)

The Rejected King

The Promised Prince

The Stolen Princess

The Forgotten Queen

The Desolate World

Famously In Love (Romantic Comedy)

Why Trey Let Me Get Away

How Jenna Became My Dilemma

The Sweet Rom "Com" Series

Commit

Compared

Complex

Complete

Christmas Books (Romantic Comedy)

Later On We'll Conspire

The Holiday Stand-In

Acknowledgments

I originally wrote this novella during Covid quarantine in 2020. My debut novel, The Promised Prince, was due to release in January of 2021, and I wanted to release a free novella before then to attract more readers for The Promised Prince. So that's how this book started.

I don't know if it was Covid or just the nature of the desolation time period, but this little novella turned out a lot darker than I was anticipating. I didn't think anyone would want to continue on with the series and read The Promised Prince after reading this book, so I shelved it. Instead, I wrote The Rejected King, which is a lot more lighthearted and fluffy--and that was probably the best decision I ever made.

After a year of writing and releasing five rom coms, I was burned out and taking a much-needed break. But this story kept popping into my head until one day I decided to open it back up. I already had 35,000 plus words in it. Granted, the writing needed a lot of help (apparently, I've grown as a writer in the two years since I shelved this one), and I had to switch back to third-person point of view, which isn't as easy as you'd think, but I wanted to give my readers who love Desolation this story. So the process of rewriting this novella began.

Thanks to Stacy, McKenna, Michelle, and Kaylen for reading the worst version of this story two years ago. Seriously. I'm sorry for that horrific mess.

Thank you to Nicole, Meredith, Michelle, Tasha, and Madi for helping me make this new version something that readers would hopefully love. And Madi, I loved your suggestions for the ending. That's all you.

Jenn Lockwood, thank you, as always, for your help with grammar and polishing the story. You were so flexible when I kept asking for a few more days, and I really appreciate it.

Thanks to my family and to Kurt. I wonder if it ever gets old being in my acknowledgments.

I'm grateful to my Heavenly Father and Jesus Christ for helping me get through my burnout and blessing me with excitement for this story.

And last but definitely not least, thank you to all my readers out there who LOVE The Desolation Series. You've stuck by my side and been patient, even when I randomly switched genres on you. I want to give you the last few Desolation books, and I promise I will. I just need time. Thanks for the support and for telling people about my books. I couldn't do it without all of my readers.

About the Author

Kortney loves all things romance. Her devotion to romance was first apparent at three-years-old when her family caught her kissing the walls (she attributes this embarrassing part of her life to her mother's affinity for watching soap operas like Days of Our Lives). Luckily, Kortney has outgrown that phase and now only kisses her husband. Most days, Kortney is your typical stay at home mom. She has five kids that keep her busy cleaning, carpooling, and cooking.

Writing books was never part of Kortney's plan. She graduated from the University of Utah with an English degree and spent a few years before motherhood teaching 7th and 8th graders how to write a book report, among other things. But after a reading slump, where no plots seemed to satisfy, Kortney pulled out her laptop and started writing the "perfect" love story...or at least she tried. Her debut novel, The Promised Prince, took four years to write, mostly because she never worked on it and didn't plan on doing anything with it.

Kortney loves warm chocolate chip cookies, clever song lyrics, the perfect romance movie, analyzing and talking about the perfect romance movie, playing card games, traveling with her family, and laughing with her husband.

Made in the USA
Las Vegas, NV
05 November 2024

11165223R00164